XMAS MARKS THE SPOT

KRISTIE KLEWES

XMAS MARKS THE SPOT

Merry Summerfield Cozy Mystery, Book 2

Kristie Klewes

OMG! Who hid a quarter of a cow in the trunk of my brother's beloved Mercedes? And what's with that spooky big X marking the spot on the beach where a man lies dead? Can my quarter-cow and the corpse possibly be connected?

Detective Bruce Carver doesn't think the body is any of my business, but someone's up to no good amid the twinkling Christmas decorations in drowsy Drizzle Bay.

I'm sure I can help, but maybe I'm too curious for my own good. Who's going to rescue me now a smelly rustler has roped me up far too close to that big white X? Not my brother Graham and his two goofy spaniels. Not old Margaret and little Pierre the poodle. Not my ex-husband, the unfaithful Duncan Skeene. I need a super-resourceful man with ... umm...muscles.

––––––––

For more information about me and my books, go to kristieklewes.com
As always, love and thanks to Philip for unfailing encouragement and computer un-snarling, and special thanks to my friends Diana Fraser and Shirley Megget who persuaded me to try writing something different.

1

AN UNFORTUNATE DISCOVERY

You never know what's lurking where you least expect it.

I finished the last bite of my toast and marmalade, slotted the plate into the dishwasher, and grabbed the spare smart-key to my brother's Mercedes because I needed to remove his golf clubs from the trunk. All good so far.

The dogs bounded into the garage with me, barking and sniffing. Goodness – maybe there was a dead rat, because something was definitely whiffy. Dust motes whirled around in the air as I operated the car's auto-open function and the lid rose. Both spaniels whirled around too, dancing on their hind legs and craning their necks for a better view.

"Down, boys!" I yelled. They get away with murder some-times. Why isn't Graham firmer with them?

And phew – the *smell* once it was open. I clutched my throat, trying not to throw up. Not a dead rat in the corner of the garage. A dead....? Ummmm? Leg of beef? In the car. All my hair stood on end. Hair was standing up on end all over the leg of beef, too, which was laid thoughtfully on a sheet of heavy plastic, so at least the carpet hadn't got soaked through. But OMG, the stink! On top was a somewhat bloody piece of cardboard with a message in bold black marker pen. BEEFY HALDANE BETTER WATCH OUT.

Who the heck was Beefy Haldane? What did he need to watch out for? Who'd put this in Graham's car? And why?

This was no way to start a beautiful summer's day in Drizzle Bay, New Zealand!

Graham is a lawyer, and was currently at a legal conference in Melbourne, Australia, which is why I could nick his Merc. I surmised Beefy Haldane was a client of his who was into something criminal. That seemed reasonable. To me, anyway. But how had anyone got an entire leg of beef into a locked car inside a locked garage on a property guarded by two uber-nosy dogs? How had they even carried it? It was enormous.

"Good dogs, good dogs," I crooned as I hauled on Manny and Dan's collars to stop them trying to eat the evidence. Eventually I got them back onto the chains attached to their kennels. They weren't keen to leave a prize like that, and continued to whine and bark and dance about with such fervor I thought they might drag the kennels behind them over the yard. In desperation I tore into the kitchen and brought out duplicate breakfasts. They fell to eating but continued to give me the evil eye for stealing such a treat.

Poor darlings – they'd been acting rather strangely for

the weekend Graham had been away – sniffing around the garage as though they suspected me of locking him in there. Given the walks I'd taken them on, and the generous meals I'd provided, this seemed less than grateful, but now I knew why.

So much for looking forward to having our rather yummy vicar, Paul McCreagh, beside me while we drove to the airport in Wellington to collect his sister. She was flying in from England for a Kiwi Christmas. Would the police let me have the car back in time? And how much of that stench could I get rid of, if so?

I'd better explain that I'm Merry Summerfield, a divorced freelance book editor, and I share the family home with Graham after our darling parents left it to us. Arnold and Sally Summerfield. They died many years too early in a nasty car crash. I try not to think about that, but of course it turns up in my brain all the time. Graham is six years older than my forty-four, and conservative beyond belief – hence his choice of a nice safe car like the Mercedes, and in the same shade of silver-gray everyone else seems to choose.

His is much more suitable than my nifty little Ford Focus for collecting a passenger who's travelled halfway around the world. She might have heaps of luggage. Her brother, Vicar Paul, certainly expected so, and as his car was temporarily out of action I'd offered to fill the gap.

Plainly I needed to contact Detective Sergeant Bruce Carver again. He of the severely bitten fingernails and overapplied cologne. Oddly, the latter might be a benefit this time because boy, that meat really ponged.

I paced to and fro outside the garage a couple of times, psyching myself up. Then, holding my breath and my cell phone, I approached the car, trying to persuade myself there was no need to be sick on the floor. I did my best to take a reasonable photo and beat a hasty retreat out into the fresh air again so I could start re-breathing. I sat on the timber garden seat for a minute or two, feeling a bit faint and shaky.

Cut it out, Merry! You weren't this bad when you found old Isobel Crombie's body a couple of months ago. And she was a human being, not a leg of beef.

But Paul was there.

And Isobel didn't smell.

Yes, having someone else for company and only the sweet scent of flowers was way preferable, but that wasn't how the cookie had crumbled for me today.

DS Carver's card was pinned up on the corkboard in the kitchen. I sent him the photo of the beef in the trunk and then rang.

And wouldn't you know it – he was instantly available instead of roaming the coast interrogating crims and leaving his phone to take messages.

"Ms Summerfield," he said in his nasal Kiwi twang. "I was just thinking about you."

I really hoped he wasn't, unless it was because of the photo.

Dismissing any other thoughts why he could be, I rushed

ahead. "Did you get that shot I sent? That's why I'm ringing. I've found a quarter of a cow in Graham's car. It still has its fur on... ummm, hide on. It's black, so maybe it's an Angus."

DS Carver cleared his throat very noisily. "Slow down, slow down, Ms Summerfield. I'm going to record this conversation if that's okay with you?"

I clutched at my long hair with my free hand, imagining him plugging things in or twiddling dials. "Yes, fine." I could hardly turn him down.

"Soooo..." he drawled. "Not to give too much away, because we've been trying to keep a lid on it, but Jim Drizzle's farm has been the subject of a couple of rustling raids. If the beast still has its hide on, that could be very helpful."

"Yes, definitely still has its hide on. Could you read that notice in my photo?"

"Loud and clear, Ms Summerfield."

I rushed on. "The thing is, I don't think it's aimed at Graham. Whoever did this laid a sheet of plastic under it to protect the car's carpet. What kind of crook bothers to do that?"

DS Carver cleared his throat again. "Have you touched anything?"

"Euw – you must be joking!"

"I'll take that as a 'no'."

"Yes, that's a no for sure. It stinks. It doesn't seem to be fly-blown, and I guess that's because the Merc's seals are good. Graham's forever going on about them." I gave a nervous laugh. "Actually, it probably *is* fly-blown by now because I left everything open to try and get rid of the smell. Insects will be streaming in there as we speak."

"Yes, yes," he muttered. I could hear his irritation from miles away. "How long since the car was used?"

"Friday. It has to be Friday because Graham flew out to Melbourne early Saturday. With another lawyer friend who's going to the same conference. Heaven help they should waste any weekday work time. They took the friend's car to the airport, so that's why Graham's is still here."

"And explains why you're phoning me instead of him. We'll need to contact him and confirm that."

"Of course you will," I agreed in a sickly sweet voice. Why did DS Carver bring out the worst in me? "But don't do it yet for a while because he'll still be asleep. Time difference between Australia and New Zealand, and all that..."

I pictured Graham peacefully snoring in his striped pajamas. I love him heaps, even though I make terrible fun of him sometimes. "He doesn't know about it," I added. "I got on to you straight away because there was no point waking him up and upsetting him. Are you going to send someone to take fingerprints? I could do with help to lift the darn thing out. It must weigh half a ton."

"Touch nothing!" DS Carver practically barked. "I'll have someone there as soon as I can."

"Good," I agreed. "I need to get it cleaned up because the vicar and I will be collecting his sister and her luggage in it this evening. She's flying in from England."

"Is she indeed?" DS Carver said in a voice dripping with

suspicion. I don't know why, because right now Heather McCreagh was probably still high over the Pacific Ocean, and she would possibly have been high over Heathrow when the beef was ladled into Graham's car.

"She's landing in Auckland about now, meeting up with an old school friend for lunch, and arriving in Wellington around five tonight."

There – that was all I knew. "I'm going to duck down to the Mini-mart and buy some air freshener because we don't seem to have any," I added. "Only be gone five minutes."

I disconnected while he was still hemming and hawing. There'd be plenty of time later to answer anything else, and for sure there'd be plenty of 'else' if I knew him.

I went outside and peered into the garage again. Some buzzy flies had already arrived, attracted no doubt by the smell of very ripe meat in the hot summer air. Oh well, too late now. I left the car open but closed the garage door. Then I pulled my exuberant hair up into a ponytail, swiped a bit of lippy on, and hid my un-made-up eyes behind my biggest, darkest sunglasses, reminding myself not to take them off while I shopped.

I locked the back door to the house and hopped into my Ford Focus. Within minutes I was in Drizzle Bay village. At nine-thirty on a Monday morning the shops were quiet. Christmas lights along their veranda edges twinkled merrily but more or less invisibly in the bright sun as I trotted past the café. Chubby, cheerful Iona Coppington was dragging some lightweight chairs out to put beside the tables she sets up each morning and pulls in again late every afternoon. "Chocolate cupcakes with caramel fudge frosting," she bellowed as I hurried by.

"Put one in a bag for me. Back in a mo," I responded, knowing I shouldn't or I'd end up the same size as her. The woman can cook, that's for sure, but I'd have to give up my toast and marmalade breakfast habit and eat something sawdusty and low-cal if I scoffed many more of her glorious treats. Sighhhh...

I wondered what sort of lingering fragrance Heather McCreagh would prefer. I dithered between Eastern Rose and French Begonia. I might not know much about gardening, but I'm pretty sure begonias have no scent in the real world. Hey-ho – marketing's a long way from reality sometimes. Those TV ads where someone throws a big chunk of butter into already-mixed cake batter crack me up each time. Me and everyone else who bakes, I suspect.

———

I DECIDED NOT to alert Graham. Why wreck his day? DS Carver would be sure to do that perfectly efficiently. Clutching the Eastern Rose air freshener, I collected and paid for my cupcake and zipped home again.

Should I tell you Drizzle Bay is named after Jim Drizzle's family farm, and not the weather? It's on the coast of New Zealand's North Island. The southern part of the North Island, to be precise. There are a couple of other small settlements nearby – Burkeville on the highway north, and Totara Flat – inland and very rural. Not a lot happens around here, and that's the way we like it.

I made sure the gate was locked behind me and headed inside. Off came the sunglasses, on went the eye make-up, and I fluffed around with my hair for a while in case there were any particularly attractive and available fingerprint men.

No, but at least everyone turned up promptly. Two white Police cars with bright blue and yellow checkerboard bands around them squealed to a flashy stop on the road outside. Overkill, in my opinion – when did we ever see *two* in Drizzle Bay? Surely they must have been coming back from an accident on the Expressway?

This caused neighbors to lean over fences, hopeful for details. People even wandered across from the beach and peered up the driveway. Some pulled out their phones and took photos, although why they thought a garage with the roller door at least halfway down and the backs of uniformed cops would make a great shot, I can't imagine.

The uniforms were followed by the Scene of Crime team who took notes, more photos, and dabbed fingerprint powder around the edges of the trunk. They stuck pieces of tape over the most promising-looking prints, peeled them off, and bagged them up. Two sturdy cops were instructed to remove the huge piece of cow by lifting the corners of the plastic sheeting so nothing gross escaped onto Graham's precious carpet. I felt sorry for them, having to get so close.

I'd opened the garage window, but that wasn't helping in the least. They dragged it out into the fresh air and the cell phone brigade went into overdrive – until the smell wafted in their direction.

Then the carpet and the lining were removed from the trunk! I hadn't expected that, but maybe there'd be some sort of evidence on it. Just as well Graham wasn't there to see his precious baby being dismantled.

One of the forensics men closed the garage door entirely so he could spray his special blood-finding chemical around and shine his light on it. Luminol – I remembered that from editing a couple of lurid thrillers for a woman called Bree Child (and I didn't think that was a clever pen name in the least). No glistening blood showed up on the floor, which was probably a relief. All in all it seemed a lot of attention for a not very large crime.

During this whole time the spaniels whined, howled, and tugged at the ends of their chains by the far fence. I've no idea how they didn't break their necks. I ambled across and gave them some pats and fondles but there was too much exciting smelly stuff happening for me to be able to calm them down much.

"What's going on?" Kaydee-Jane Simmons demanded from part way up the plum tree next door. The spaniels renewed their chorus of annoyance.

"Are you safe up there?" I asked. "Why aren't you at school?"

"Got a cold," she said, sniffing to prove it.

"Then you should be inside in bed."

She looked at me with the withering gaze of a six-year-old who knows everything. "Mummy says it's warmer out here."

And she wouldn't be interrupting Mummy Rochelle's TV programs outside, would she! Kaydee-Jane's mother is not industrious, enterprising, or particularly maternal. If she can stay sitting, she does. By contrast her grandmother is a gem.

"So what's going on?" the little girl demanded again.

"Someone broke into Graham's car."

"What did they break?"

"The lock." Which probably wasn't true, because I'd seen no damage.

"Have the crooks gone?"

"Absolutely," I assured her.

She looked disappointed, so I waved a firm goodbye and went to check if anyone wanted a cup of tea or coffee yet. No.

A bit of eavesdropping followed as I weeded the pots either side of the now-open-again garage door – really the only gardening I bother with, and I heard nothing the least bit illuminating. After the team left I went back into the house and tied my hair in a pony-tail again. The beach gawpers returned to their sand.

DS Carver eventually arrived in his anonymous Police-issue sedan. He had Detective Marion Wick with him again – she of the huge, attractive eyes and unfairly slim body.

Why do some people have all the luck? She could probably eat Iona's cupcakes every day of the year and never put on an ounce. (Of course she might go running, too, and spend a heap of time at the gym.)

"Tea or coffee?" I asked. Once again I was turned down so I led them through to the big front sitting room with its view out over the sea. We went around and around in circles with the questions because I really couldn't tell them much more than what I'd reported on the phone, and I'd already given them Graham's cell phone number so they could ring him.

"Who's this Beefy Haldane?" I asked when DS Carver finally stopped to draw breath.

"Ah," he said unhelpfully.

"Something to do with the cattle rustling?" (Or possibly sheep rustling for all I knew.)

"Connected. Connected," he conceded while Detective Wick opened her eyes even wider.

"Connected to Graham as well?" I pressed.

"It's too early to know," DS Carver stated, resting his elbows on his knees and leaning further toward me. I edged away to avoid the cologne, which even toward the end of the morning was still super strong.

Marion Wick smelled fantastic by comparison. Once again I imagined her cuddled up to John Bonnington from the Burkeville Bar and Café with him sniffing her neck and dropping kisses down the front of her shirt. I had no actual evidence of such a liaison, but plenty of suspicions.

"Well, he's got to be connected somehow, doesn't he?" I suggested. "Otherwise, why choose Graham's car? And how did anyone unlock the garage, unlock the car, avoid making the dogs suspicious, and then lock everything up again? In fact it might have been two people because that meat weighed a ton."

DS Carver chewed the inside of his cheek for a few seconds. "We have a theory... and *only* a theory at this time... that the car may have been tampered with in the parking lot at his place of work. On Friday, perhaps."

Huh! Not so stupid after all.

"But keep that to yourself please, Ms Summerfield. Currently we have no reason to believe your brother is involved in anything illegal."

I'm sure my eyes shot so wide open they became at least as large as Marion Wick's. "I certainly hope not!" I said in my best huffy tone. "He's a lawyer. He doesn't need extra money, and he's boringly trustworthy." I tossed my head and my pony-tail whacked a china cat off the bookshelf behind me. "For what it's worth, I like your parking lot theory. I would have heard the dogs if it had been done here." I picked the cat up. Sadly it was still unbroken. I'd given it to my mother for Christmas when I was a child, and it was kind of too big a memory to throw out while it remained whole.

"You haven't been away on any of your pet-minding assignments?" Detective Wick asked, narrowing her eyes at the ugly cat.

"This week I'm pet-minding right here at home," I snapped, adding a sniff to emphasize that fact.

There didn't seem to be much more to say on either side so they were gone before lunchtime. I slipped into the garage, sprayed another dose of Eastern Rose inside the car, and retired, coughing, to let the spaniels off their chains now there'd be no-one else to chase. Then, finding some common sense at last, I drove the Merc out of the garage, opened all the windows and the trunk, and let the summer sea breeze flow through. It was only then I noticed the beef was no longer in the middle of the driveway. Had the Police taken it as evidence? I decided it was more likely they'd dropped it off at the local landfill for me. What darlings!

———

"HI, PAUL," I said as the vicar pulled his front door closed later that afternoon and the shiny brass knocker bounced with a bang on the equally shiny striker plate fixed to the glossy red enamel paint. He's painted the church railings, too, and old Peggy Legget's back porch. Jasper Hornbeam is the village's 'official' handyman, but Paul McCreagh likes doing practical jobs too, as long as he can fly under the radar. They sometimes team up and I think they both enjoy the DIY and the company.

I looked up at the sky and wrinkled my nose. "Our fine day seems to be clouding over. It'll be a pity if Heather's first sight of Drizzle Bay is through actual drizzle."

Paul's far too tempting for a man of God. There's at least six feet of him, topped by a thatch of short wavy dark hair which matches his mobile eyebrows and dark brown eyes.

He laughed at my 'drizzle' comment. He's too kind not to. "Do I look okay?" he asked.

Any other man would be fishing for compliments but I'm sure he simply wanted assurance his sister would approve of his appearance. Dark gray trousers, sage green shirt, shiny black shoes. Totally respectable, and not a hint of churchiness about him. Interesting.

"Very impressive," I assured him. "You look exactly right for Graham's posh car. Hop in, because I have a ridiculous story to tell you."

He raised one of the aforementioned eyebrows before pulling the passenger door open and settling into the leather-upholstered seat. He sniffed. "Does your brother like roses?"

I grinned as I navigated out into the road. It's a beautiful car to drive but I was conscious of its size, not to mention its price tag. "That's part of the ridiculous story. I went out to the garage early this morning to remove Graham's golf clubs so there'd be plenty of room for Heather's luggage and instead I found a quarter of a cow and a threatening notice."

I glanced over briefly to see how he'd taken that.

"Good grief woman, you attract trouble," he said in a surprisingly mild tone. "I'm guessing the threatening notice wasn't meant for you, though? Why would anyone have it in for Graham?"

"It wasn't meant for Graham, either. Have you come across anyone called Beefy Haldane?"

I saw him swallow. "Dammit," he said. "He's not a good

person to know, Merry. A real loner. A wild man. And I mean that in the sense of a man who lives miles away from civilization and seems to live only by his own rules."

The lights on the railway crossing ahead of us started to flash, and as I drew nearer the frantic 'ding-ding-ding' of the warning signal became audible. Once I'd brought the big quiet car to a halt I turned to Paul and said, "It wasn't from this Beefy person to Graham. It was telling Beefy to watch out, but someone had broken into Graham's car and left it there."

I found the photo on my phone and passed it over to him while we were stopped. "Graham's in Melbourne. That's why I could pinch his car when yours packed up. I tried ringing him, but I timed it really badly because he was on the point of giving a speech. I'd already called the cops and it's in their hands now." I looked at Paul more closely. "So how do you know Beefy Haldane? A loner and a wild man? He doesn't sound like a church-goer."

Paul remained silent for a few seconds and then said with obvious reluctance, "There was an incident out at my Totara Flat church a few weeks ago. He smashed the lock with the big stone we use as a door-stop. There's no money kept there. The old chap who gives me a hand with the lawns called me and said there was a madman inside."

I drew a sharp breath at that. "And I suppose you tore off on your own to investigate?"

He jerked a shoulder. "I expected a teenager with a bad attitude. Instead I found a man who looked more like a bear

– all hair and incoherent growls. My church stank of cannabis, and he'd located the communion wine, too. All gone – not that there was much of it. He was waving a rifle around and taking pot-shots at the rafters."

For the second time that day my gorge rose and I thought I might be sick. "Paul!" I exclaimed. "He could have killed you."

"Yes," he agreed, and the corners of his mouth pulled up in the faintest of grins. "But I do have heavenly protection, you know."

"Does that work with drunken madmen?"

He nodded very slowly. "There are some benefits to having been a chaplain in Afghanistan, Merry. We had a long talk about guns."

I know my eyebrows rose. I almost choked, huffing in a surprised breath and having to cough a couple of times.

"He was very keen to get his hands on a military style assault rifle now they've changed the gun laws," Paul continued. "Of course I have no idea how to get one," – he rolled his eyes at me – "but I managed to keep him talking until he calmed down, came to his senses somewhat, and staggered out. He took off across the open countryside on the muddiest motorbike you ever saw."

"Thank heavens for that."

Paul rubbed a hand across his mouth. "There's one other thing; Roddy."

At that moment the freight train reached the level crossing and roared across, making further conversation impossible until it had rattled by. Even the superior sound-proofing of the Merc wasn't a match for a diesel electric engine at full speed and its following collection of rushing, clanking flat-beds with multi-colored shipping containers and piles of de-barked logs from the forests further north. Paul and I looked at each other with apologetic shrugs, unable to continue until we could hear each other again.

It gave me plenty of time to remember Roddy. The poor man's surname was Whitebottom. I've heard of Winterbottoms, which are pretty bad, and Ramsbottoms, which aren't much better, but Roddy's name took the cake. He'd come to Paul for counseling in Afghanistan when his promiscuous behavior got him into trouble, had read more into Paul's concern than religious care, and turned into a real nuisance. Turned up in Drizzle Bay, too, and had to be gently but firmly discouraged.

Finally the signal gave up its frantic dinging and the lights stopped flashing.

"We had to get a few holes in the roof mended," Paul said. "Good thing it was corrugated metal and not hundred-year-old slates or Marseilles tiles. We'd have had a job matching those."

I accelerated smoothly away and onto the main highway. The rear-view mirror told me there were plenty more vehicles following us. It's amazing how traffic builds up, even in such a small place. "So he took off on a motorbike and you were okay?" I was much more interested in Paul's safety than the state of the church roof.

"I called the police of course, but as he wasn't on a public road and seemed to be heading for the hills, I think they concluded he'd be safely out of everyone's way for a while."

"And was he – um – 'known to the police' as they say?"

Paul nodded. "Known many times over. As a nuisance rather than a criminal, but the gun got them rattled. I don't think they'd tied him to firearms before."

I wasn't letting him get away with raising a topic like troublemaker Roddy and then dropping it. "Yes, so what about Roddy?"

If ever I'd seen a man who didn't want to talk about something, here he was.

He cleared his throat, stayed silent for a while, and finally said, "It turned out Beefy Haldane was who Roddy went bush with."

"Well, they'll make a great pair," I said unkindly. "A hairy bear and your delicate friend."

"*Not* my friend," Paul grated. "He's a good shot, though. And a mischief maker. I don't imagine they're up to any good together."

I gnawed on my bottom lip. "There was nothing about the church break-in in any of the news feeds."

"No. They told me they thought he was part of something bigger and they wanted to stay quiet about it for a while."

I immediately thought of the possible rustling on Jim Drizzle's farm. Lord Drizzle, to be correct. As the last surviving member of a noble old English family he's inherited the title, but seems a lot happier being a New Zealand farmer than an English lord. He does pop over to England periodically though and do a bit of voting in the House of Lords – no doubt on matters that influence the sale and importation of the beef and lamb he produces.

I looked sideways and caught Paul's eye. "Well, I'm swearing you to silence on this, but I dug a little nugget out of DS Carver this morning. They're investigating some local rustling. Part of a cow left in Graham's car... beef of course... and a warning message for Beefy Haldane. Possible, you reckon?"

His eyes narrowed. "Rustling? Good grief – are we in the Wild West?" He reached up and adjusted his sun visor against the bright overcast sky. "I wouldn't put it past them though."

We were coming up to a notorious bend where the Police often waited for speedsters. Sure enough they were there again, right as the lime green and black 'boy-racer' car that had been following me too closely chose to overtake with a great roar and a cloud of stinky smoke. I hope they got a good shot of its registration plate.

"Pack of fools," I muttered.

Paul nodded, and then surprised me by grinning. "We were all young once."

"I was never *that* young," I protested.

"I'm sure you were a very proper young lady," he said, smile undimmed.

Not that proper either, I couldn't help thinking.

I turned the ventilation up a notch in the hope it would

hurry the departure of the cloying rosy fragrance and the new whiff of stinky smoke. And possibly cool down any extra pink in my cheeks. "I would have been trying to evade the clutches of Duncan Skeene at that age. And not entirely succeeding."

"Your barely lamented ex?" His gaze sharpened and I wondered, not for the first time, if Paul was interested in me as more than a friend. I also wondered if I'd ever make a suitable wife for a vicar. They might not be allowed to marry anyone who's been divorced – another thing I needed to Google, although Prince Harry now has his Meghan…

And I'm probably getting way ahead of myself here.

2

HEATHER FOR CHRISTMAS

"So TELL me more about your sister," I suggested as we glided along. "Older or younger than you? Single or married?" I was presuming single because there'd been no mention of children coming with her. We'd have needed to hire a minibus if so because I wasn't silly enough to invite a selection of small fractious English children to romp all over Graham's pale gray leather upholstery and scuff it with shoe buckles or the studs and zippers on trendy jeans.

In fact there'd been virtually no mention of a sister at all in the short time I'd known Paul. It was only by chance that he'd been painting the church railings when I stopped to put a notice on the community board about my new live-in pet-minding services. He'd looked nothing like a vicar on that occasion, and to be honest I'd been ogling the tanned legs on the handsome handyman as I drew nearer, and got one heck of a fright to find it was him under the hat. Then we'd had the misfortune to discover Isobel's body sprawled in the aisle of his church – more of a misfortune for her than us, of course – which led rapidly to my first pet- minding assignment and more of Paul's company.

"Two years younger," he said. "And widowed. I'm hoping this trip to New Zealand will cheer her up a bit."

"She doesn't have kids, does she?"

"No children, more's the pity. It would have given her a distraction from Robert's death. She's been moldering away for more than a year now. I know that probably seems harsh but it's how our mother describes her to me."

"Moldering," I repeated. "Sounds so sad."

"Sad and a bit self-indulgent, according to Mother."

I shot a sharp glance in his direction. "Does Mother still have a husband? Is she in any fit state to judge sorrow?"

(To be honest, I'd asked Jim Drizzle about Paul's politician father, but I wasn't admitting that to him.)

"No, I no longer have a father," Paul said, although he had the good grace to attach a smile to his somewhat snarky reply.

Hmmm. So the sister would be around forty and unhappy. She didn't sound the ideal guest for our gentle vicar who'd been 'sent to the colonies' to try and recover from the PTSD he'd sustained as a result of his work in Afghanistan.

I signaled to pull out, and overtook an elderly VW Beetle. "It'll be different for her to have a summertime Christmas instead of a winter one. What are her interests? How are you going to occupy her – apart from some time on the beach?"

Paul did that thing men sometimes do when they're thinking... scraping his forefinger and thumb up and down over the bristles on his chin, pursing his lips, and consider- ing. "She's a keen golfer," he said. "Although there's no way she'll have bought her clubs with her. The excess baggage charge would be horrendous."

"They'd fit in the back if she has," I assured him. "Graham mostly kept his there. But either he'd deliberately taken them out so there'd be room for the beef – which is ridiculous – or he'd decided to have a go with the Auto Vac because I found them leaning against the garage wall. Maybe she could borrow his? Or do they have bags and clubs they hire out?"

Paul gnawed on the inside of his cheek, still plainly deep in thought, and probably no longer about golf. "She likes cooking. Mother was trying to get her to apply for that Bake-off program on TV but she wouldn't. Last time, while Robert was still alive, she was busting to."

"Well, at least you'll be well fed while she's staying. Maybe she could see if Iona at the café needs a hand with any Christmas goodies?"

He stroked his chin some more while he thought about that. "She used to enjoy hiking and rambling," he finally added. "The English countryside is a lot easier than some of the bush tracks here, but we could try that."

We? Was I included? Or did he mean him and his sister?

"Sounds a great idea," I said, also giving nothing away. I decided to buy some suitable new shoes, in case. My ratty old sneakers were only good for the garden now and for sure wouldn't be any use for serious tramping.

Tramping – hmmm. Kiwi. Rambling sounded English, and I'm sure Americans hiked. You have to watch out for things like that when you're a freelance editor. That's what I really do for my living – the live-in pet-minding is an recent added extra to give me some privacy away from Graham.

Oh well – it would be a calorie-burning walk in the fresh air with trees and views, whatever we called it. I noted that Paul was already referring to our vast native forests as 'bush'. A tame name for something that included majestic kauri trees sometimes two or three thousand years old and of such a size you gasp out loud when you first see them.

We drove on, mostly in companionable silence. I suspected Paul was a bit worried about the extent of Heather's 'moldering'. I didn't like to ask, but I pictured his mother as one of those efficient tweedy ladies who bossed English villages around. Always on a committee organizing something. Or perhaps taking a recalcitrant family member in hand.

Poor Heather. If she was truly depressed then a few weeks of summer weather and time away from her bossy parent might help but it wouldn't be any guarantee of a cure. She probably needed a new man to replace all the sadness of losing her old one. Er – her late husband.

I was sure a new man would cheer *me* up heaps – and I was already pretty contented.

After nosing around the airport for a while I found a short-term park beside a pillar which several people had already scraped. I proceeded with care and managed to shoe-horn the car into it.

Paul and I walked into the main concourse with plenty of time to spare before Heather was due to land. He paused beside the enormous glass window that gave a ring-side view of the take-offs and landings. "I always thought that job looked like fun" he said, nodding towards the orange jack-eted men zooming about in little jeeps towing trolleys loaded with baggage.

"I always thought *that* job would be fun," I said pointing to the huge sculpture of the spooky Gollum leering down at us from high up on the wall.

Paul looked up and smiled. "International visitors certainly get to hear about New Zealand's connection to the Lord of the Rings film trilogy." His brows drew together. "Did you really want to be an artist instead of a book editor?"

I glanced across to where an eagle, so large a full-sized human witch was perched between its massive wings, hung. "Wouldn't have had the talent. I was always good with words and my life just went in that direction."

We'd no sooner settled ourselves with a coffee and a cupcake each (yes, I admit it, my second high-calorie treat for the day) than my handbag started playing 'Jingle Bells'. What can I say? I enjoy messing with my cell phone's ringtones, and that had seemed a good choice for December. Paul grinned, and I scrambled to grab it before too many people around us started laughing at my choice.

It was Detective Wick of the Photo-shopped eyes. "Ms Summerfield – just another couple of questions if you don't mind?"

"No probs," I said, which might have been a bit casual given the situation because she went on to ask how many smart-keys there were to Graham's car.

"Two as far as I know. There's the one always in his suit pocket or on his desk, and there's another on a hook inside one of the kitchen cupboards, although it's rarely used."

"So that's how you gained access to the car, and found the er...?"

"Leg of beef," I offered helpfully. Of course it was. "Yes." What was she really getting at?

"And you've never noticed it missing?"

Paul's eyebrows were climbing his forehead as he stirred the sugar into his coffee.

"No, I've never noticed it missing, but I don't look for it very often. It's just... there. I'm much more concerned to know where my own keys are. "

"So it could have been removed from the kitchen cupboard and replaced again without you noticing?"

I changed my phone to the other hand. Paul had sprinkled the little paper tube of sugar into my coffee so I picked up my teaspoon and started to stir. "Yes, I suppose so, but it's most unlikely. The house is often locked if I'm there working on my own, and it's *always* locked if Graham's at work and I'm not there."

"*Often* locked?"

"There are two dogs running free on the property. It's well fenced and has a gate, and the dogs are inside that gate with me. They bark at strangers. I don't feel the need to lock it up like Fort Knox."

She seemed to be considering that because it was a while before she asked, "Ms Summerfield, who else would know about the key in the kitchen cupboard?"

Oh, this was getting silly! "No-one. Why would they? We don't have visitors who open and shut the kitchen cupboards to see what's in them."

I closed my eyes and found Paul biting into his cupcake when I opened them.

"Tradespeople or cleaning staff perhaps?" She was definitely thorough.

I gave it a few seconds' thought. "No tradespeople for ages. An electrician back in June or July because the garage and porch lights were playing up. I don't expect he looked in the kitchen cupboards. You saw it was quite an old house, and the switchboard with all the circuit-breaker thingies is in the kitchen. But it's up above the cupboards. You don't need to open any of them to get to it."

"And who was the electrician, Ms Summerfield?"

I gritted my teeth. "Evan Sutcliffe of Sutcliffe Electrical. We've used him before."

"And cleaners?"

"It wouldn't be her. She was useless. Barely cleaned anything. Certainly didn't bother opening any cupboard doors. I went back to doing it myself again." I set the teaspoon down on my saucer with a clatter, hoping Detective Wick might hear it and deduce I was in a social situation and could do without her questions.

"And that was...?"

I sighed. "Our next door neighbor, Rochelle Simmons. Or at least she's the grown-up daughter of our next door neighbor. Useless girl. Had a baby very young. No husband. Her mother was trying to find work for her. So when Nancy asked – that's the mother – I said we'd give Rochelle two hours' housework each week as a favor. Just the floors really." I stopped talking for a moment and sipped my coffee while it was still hot enough. "And she was so unenthusiastic we let her go after a few weeks. Sighs of relief all round, I suspect. She brought her cute wee daughter with her the last time. School holidays. Kaydee-Jane. *She* has a lot more spark than her mother."

"And you've no feeling any of the cupboards were opened?"

I scoffed at that. "Only the one in the utility room where we keep the vacuum cleaner and broom and so on. And not with any enthusiasm."

"And the little girl wouldn't have gone exploring?"

I gave my coffee another stir. "Even if she had, she couldn't have reached that key. Kaydee-Jane is six. I doubt she comes to the top of the kitchen counter. The key is in a bank of cupboards above that. Miles above her head. Almost miles above mine. I have to reach up for it, so no – not a chance."

I noticed Paul checking his watch and decided I'd had enough of Marion Wick. "I'm sorry, but I think the flight I'm waiting for has just landed. I need to go and meet someone."

"Thanks again," she said breezily. "We know where to find you." And disconnected.

I shrugged at Paul. "Marion Wick. They're trying to work out how anyone else got into Graham's car. Is it time we went up to Arrivals?"

"No – another ten minutes or so. Just buying you time to enjoy your coffee."

I smiled gratefully. Nice man. He needed a wife to enjoy life with.

———

HEATHER WAS BEAUTIFUL. As blonde as Paul was dark. Blonder than me, and paler-skinned, although I had to remember she'd just arrived from the middle of an English winter. Absolutely an English rose, and rather a droopy one after the long flight.

I was interested to hear how Paul introduced me once he released her from an enthusiastic hug and a kiss on the cheek. Was I a friend? A special friend? A parishioner?

"Heather, this is Merry Summerfield who's been kind enough to give us a ride home."

Well, that didn't tell her much! Or me.

"There's plenty of room in the car for luggage," I said, still vaguely wondering about golf clubs, and slightly miffed at Paul's lack of description.

"Brought the minimum," she said, yawning and then apologizing. "Only two to collect, and neither huge." She grasped the handle of her wheelie cabin bag. It looked to be right up to the size limit, but I guess a flight halfway around the world is a different proposition from just an hour between Wellington and Auckland.

We followed the queue of other arrivals and greeters to the baggage claim area. Garlands of tinsel and shiny baubles hung from the walls and Christmas music swelled from concealed speakers. I privately thought some lovely Maori songs would have made a nice welcome, but then again it would have sounded rude chopping into them with crackly announcements. Paul commandeered a trolley, and ten or so minutes later we were rolling out toward the car. Heather shrugged off her jacket the moment we hit the open air. "That's better," she said, draping it around her cabin bag handle, flexing her shoulders, and drawing in a deep breath. "I *so* needed to get away to somewhere different."

"And away from Mother?" Paul suggested.

"You have no idea."

He gave a grim laugh. "I probably have, you know."

Heather linked her arm through his. "Maybe you do at that, Paul-James."

Paul-James? I liked that.

"So I thought we might have dinner at a local bistro to welcome you," he said as we reached the car.

Heather looked up at him and gave her head a slow shake. "I was thinking a pot of tea, a slice of toast, and early to bed would be perfect."

I saw disappointment on Paul's face and quickly countered with, "Or brunch tomorrow at the Burkeville, which would really be better because the weather was closing in when we left. Their courtyard is lovely on a fine morning."

He gave a wry smile and conceded defeat as I opened the trunk to stow the luggage away. I'd lined it with a colorful old Persian hearth mat in lieu of the carpet the Police had in their care. His smile grew broader at the unlikely sight. "Beans on that toast?" he asked Heather.

"Too much," she murmured. "A scrape of honey? Something light. It feels like I've been sitting in planes forever, and there's constant food, plus my lunch in Auckland."

Yes, it's a long trip all the way from England to New Zealand, and it sounded as though she'd flown direct.

"Okay, brunch tomorrow at the Burkeville if it's fine," he agreed.

"I'd better bring the dogs after leaving them alone this afternoon," I inserted. "Which will be fine in my smaller car without luggage because they'd go mad in this one with the smell." I mentally slapped myself on the head. "Unless you two want some time alone, seeing Heather's only just arrived?" I make such stupid assumptions sometimes!

"No," they said in unison, so I hoped they meant it.

"Roses?" Heather asked, raising her head and sniffing as she slid into the passenger side.

"Something like that," I agreed. "It wasn't so rosy this morning."

Paul pulled the back door closed after him and the snick of seatbelts followed. "You sure we'll all fit in yours?"

"No problem if I take the parcel shelf out." I concentrated on getting past that threatening pillar and then we threaded our way through the lanes to where the pay machines were. Heather spent the drive peering around, starting with the new air traffic control tower at the airport. There's no polite way of saying this: Wellington can be a very windy place, set as it is on the edge of the water dividing two mountainous islands. The air fairly whistles by sometimes, and the new tower has been built so it leans into the prevailing wind by a jokey twelve degrees.

"Look!" she gasped, pointing to it across the other side of the runway. Paul and I laughed at her reaction. Yes, it's spectacular – the famous Leaning Tower of Pisa leans by only four degrees. At least the Wellington one has proper foundations.

The hills around the harbor rose steep and dark, moody and dramatic as clouds drifted across the tops and swirled around the gullies. The water glittered gray and silver with reflections. Very small yachts – maybe an after-school class – wove around each other close to one of the sailing clubs.

Heather pointed to a group of houses perched high up

one of the ridges. "I can't believe some of the places they've built. The views must be fantastic."

"Have we got time for a trip up to the top of Mount Victoria?" I asked Paul.

"Be nicer on a better day." I saw his smile in the rear-view mirror. "A future treat?"

We drove on, through the city, onto the multi-lane highway that skirts the harbor, and up through the steep Ngauranga Gorge – a multi-lane engineering miracle cut through rocky hills. In no time we were out past suburbia and heading home. Paul provided commentary and answers. Sure enough, we arrived in Drizzle Bay in drizzle.

———

NEXT MORNING at 9.30 Paul's beautiful BBC accent greeted me when I'd stopped my phone playing 'Jingle Bells'. "Merry – sorry about this. Heather's still deep in the Land of Nod. She grunted, rolled over, demanded I closed her curtains again, and begged for the morning in bed." I heard the fond smile in his voice. "As the weather's still looking dodgy, I gave in without too much discussion. Can we try again tomorrow?"

Oh goody, I was all dressed and made up for an outing that wasn't going to happen.

"Of course, Paul," I replied with the utmost graciousness. "That was a really long flight for her. Brunch will be much nicer on a sunny morning, anyway."

"Are you free tomorrow? Wednesday?" There was pleasing hope in his question.

"You know me. I make my own hours." I hesitated for a couple of seconds. "I doubt she's one of yours but are you acquainted with Levana Lowenstein?"

Paul made a considering type of noise. Quite a sexy rumble, actually. "Don't think so."

"As we're not going out to the Burkeville you can think of me taking a second pass through her cheese and yoghurt recipes with accompanying wartime memories."

"Ah," he said.

"These were dictated several years ago to her grand-daughter, Rebecca, who recorded them and has been trying to arrange them into a book. She's no writer, let me tell you!"

Paul chuckled, damn him. "Bad luck. I'll leave you to that happy task, then," he said. "By the way, you might like to know you're the inspiration for this Sunday's sermon."

Surely not! How could I be?

"What do you make of 'God, who at sundry times and in divers manners spake in time past unto the fathers by the prophets'?"

"Umm?" I made nothing much at all, but how was I going to tell him that?

"Hebrews Chapter One." Paul's tone was gently teasing. "It's a lot simpler these days. There are so many versions, but here's one I like. 'In the past God spoke to our ancestors through the prophets at many times and in various ways.' Properly edited, you might say."

I swallowed. "Certainly easier to understand. I wouldn't need to take my metaphorical red pencil to that."

"And it continues, 'But in these last days He has spoken to us by his Son, whom He appointed heir of all things, and through whom also He made the universe.' Lovely words, aren't they? I think I'll use them as a demonstration that His wisdom is now more accessible than it ever used to be."

I swallowed. "You might get a few quibbles from the scientists who think they know how the universe was made."

Paul knew I was teasing him. "Good thing I don't have many scientists in my congregations," he said. "Thanks for understanding." And he disconnected.

Well, understanding about not going to the Burkeville, anyway. I was less sure about the ancestors and the prophets, but it wouldn't hurt me to grab one of the newer versions of the Bible and have a read. Get more on his wavelength, so to speak.

As I was now sadly not brunching at the Burkeville, I made some toast, heavy on the marmalade, decided the dogs were getting plenty of exercise running around the wet yard so didn't need a walk yet, and opened up my laptop. Bliss oh joy – food rationing and turnip growing.

I really wasn't in the mood. A good goss with Lurline always cheers me up so I gave her a call instead. She meets a lot of people through the animal shelter. Might she have picked up anything about rustling in the Drizzle Bay area? Mindful of Bruce Carver's request not to spread the leg of beef news around, I started with the weather after the greetings were done. "Isn't it awful? The rain's driving in against my office windows and making it really hard to concentrate. How's everything with you?"

She made a scoffing noise. "Merry Summerfield – you can't get away with talking about the weather when the Police have been hanging around your garage. What on earth's been going on there?"

Busted. I wriggled in my chair. "Well I'm sworn to secrecy on some of it, because of 'on-going investigations', as they say, but someone parked a leg of beef in the trunk of Graham's car. Two nice young constables dragged it out and put it on the driveway, and half the beach took photos."

"Not so secret, then," she said. I heard the teasing smile in her voice.

"Not that part, no. But..."

"Spit it out."

"Well, I'm wondering..."

"Yeeees...?"

"If you've had any dodgy types in there, looking for hunting dogs, maybe? I don't know, but something big and scary that could be used to round up cattle?"

"Illegally, you mean?" No flies on Lurline.

"Probably. Someone who's bred and raised a fine cattle beast isn't going to butcher it and put some in a car for a joke. It has to be stolen."

"Rustled?"

Well, she'd said it so I didn't have to. "Yes, I suppose. Have you heard anything?"

"Nothing... concrete..." I heard definite hesitation in her voice.

"Has Bruce Carver been asking?"

"Yes. His off-sider, anyway. That Wick woman."

I snorted at her description. "She's pleasant enough."

Lurline sighed. "But those legs. Those eyes. Not fair."

I had to agree. I also had to earn a living, so after a bit more chat I excused myself and started reading and high-lighting and commenting, losing myself in my work until I noticed leaves sparkling in watery sunshine and the clouds evaporating.

I sat up straighter, worked my arms to and fro like a demented duck attempting takeoff, and made sure the file was saved. Then I staggered to my feet, desperate for coffee.

Must not sit for so long at a time. Need to do more exercise. Drink more water. Yeah - it's you I'm talking to, Merry.

If I was taking the spaniels for a walk I could get back to Lurline again and see if she had any dogs of moderate size to join us. This would take me conveniently close to Iona's delicious date scones and peanut crunch bars, always supposing other people hadn't already bought them all for lunch.

"Drizzle Bay Animal Shelter," she replied crisply.

"It's me again. Got any smaller dogs you want walked? I'm taking the spaniels out soon and can cope with one more."

"Just the person I need," she said. "Yes. Very small. A cute little mini-dachshund called Theo, according to his tag. Found wandering, but was definitely someone's pet."

"Not microchipped?"

Lurline made a scoffing noise. "I can't imagine why not. It'd cost the owner a lot less than the dog."

"Okay, and if I'm passing by Iona's on my way, is there anything you'd like me to bring you? Date scone? Blueberry muffin?"

"I'd kill for something chocolatey."

"Leave it to me," I said. "Be there in thirty minutes."

And so the day whizzed by in a jumble of editing, dog-walking, a vegie stir-fry and some passionfruit ice-cream (not on the same plate) for dinner, and an episode of Married at First Sight – also something I don't get a lot of if Graham is home. Well, to be honest I mostly watch it well away from his snorts and eye-rolling on the privacy of my laptop.

It had been a nice day, and tomorrow was definitely going to be fine. Brunch at the Burkeville looked like a sure thing.

———

THE SPANIELS DIDN'T SEE why they had to sit behind the back seat, but any ride is a treat as far as they're concerned so they acted puzzled but pleased when I bundled them in on Wednesday and set off for the vicarage in my good jeans and a watermelon-pink blouse.

Daniel the spaniel. And Manual the spaniel. Yes. Named by Kaydee-Jane, the little girl from the plum tree next door who wanted nothing to do with 'Manuel' as a possible name because 'Man-well' didn't rhyme with spaniel.

Paul had reverted to vicar mode and had his dog collar on today. Heather looked a lot fresher and less rumpled in a mint green and white T-shirt and white capris. The wet weather was nothing but a memory and today Drizzle Bay was at its sparkling summer best.

"So did you tell her?" I asked Paul as soon as we were underway. I could see him trying to avoid the dogs' attention from their den behind the back seat.

Heather glanced across and I kept my eyes on the road. "Me?" she asked.

"Yes, you. Did Paul tell you about the leg of beef?"

She laid a hand on my arm. "You poor thing! That must have been disgusting to find."

"Which was why the car smelled rather rosy. You've arrived at an exciting time – right in the middle of a crime wave, it would seem."

Paul guffawed from the rear seat. "It's not a wave until they find the other three quarters."

"Euw!" Heather and I exclaimed in unison.

"Do you want me to tie those dogs to the side rails?" I asked. I could see they were giving him affectionate nudges and licks from over the back of the seat.

Paul shook his head. "They'll settle in a minute. Any more from the Police?"

"No. And I can do without DS Carver's disgusting cologne." I looked across at Heather as we slowed for an intersection. "That man just reeks of it. He's a lot worse than my brother's car. Anyway, did you sleep well?"

"Out like a light. And most of yesterday as well."

"I had to wake her up this morning or we'd never have been ready," Paul said.

"So you've no idea who did it?" Heather asked.

I shrugged. "Or *how*. It was such a huge chunk of meat I can't imagine one person carrying it."

"Well, this is exciting! I thought I was going to be mooching around, mostly on my own, doing the occasional good deed with 'brother dear', and trying not to get sunburned." Heather rubbed her hands together and sent me a gleeful smile.

"But," said Paul from the back seat, "You have to remember this is serious, Heather. I've met the chap the message was aimed at, and he's a nasty piece of work."

"Yes, darling." She turned away and gave her attention to the view, which I must say is pretty spectacular on a fine day. The sun poured down over acres of blue sea, and there was enough breeze to whip spray off the tops of the waves. "So is that pampas grass?" she asked me as we drove past some big clumps with tall feathery tassels.

"Toe toe, or toi toi. That's the true Kiwi version because it's flowering before Christmas. A bit smaller than pampas, which is pinker, bigger, later, and a real problem to get rid of sometimes. Those stems are fun for kids to run around with – until the seedy fluff all starts shedding."

Paul cleared his throat, apparently wanting to show he was right at home. "The trees with the red blooms are pohutukawa. There are some around the church, too. New Zealand Christmas trees."

Heather gave a big yawn and stretched both arms out toward the windscreen. "I really can't believe Christmas is anywhere near. A picnic on the beach when I'm used to being bundled up in winter woollies and seeing snow falling outside? Doesn't seem real."

I switched on the radio and 'Jingle Bell Rock' filled the car. "Real," I said, turning it off again as the spaniels threw back their heads and joined in with joyful howls. "Someone should write some new Christmas songs."

"Nothing wrong with the old ones," Paul said, surprising me by suddenly launching into 'We Three Kings of Orient Are'. His voice rang deep and true, and within seconds Heather had joined in. Her sweet soprano dipped and soared, and Manual and Daniel took this as an invitation to howl along, too. I glanced in the rear-view mirror. Paul's eyes were closed, and the spaniels' heads were once again thrown back in bliss. I caught Heather's eye, and grinned. "Musical family?" I mouthed.

She nodded and kept singing. We arrived at the Burkeville Bar and Café a few minutes later. By then, even I was humming along – and beating time on the steering wheel with one hand.

There were several other cars in evidence, so I slid the Focus into a vacant space and braked. "Paul – can you grab their leads, please?" I asked before we had any doors open. The last thing we needed was two spaniels dashing around the main highway unrestrained. Paul swiveled in his seat and groped about while Manny and Dan tried to lick him to death.

"Yep – all safe," he said after a bit more wrestling, so Heather and I got out and I went to the back hatch to take over. Spaniels can be stupid dogs. Lovely natures, but sometimes with no regard for their own safety. They were soon tied to the dog post just inside the café's courtyard and they immediately fell to drinking from the water bowl there.

We ambled in to inspect the blackboard menu to check out what was on offer.

John Bonnington stood behind the counter, all muscles and man-bun. John is a surfer, and to see him slicing across the waves, bare-chested, long hair streaming behind him, is absolutely no hardship. He nodded to Paul, winked at me, and then fixed his total attention on Heather. As Paul was showing no signs of introducing her, I thought I'd better do the honors.

"Heather, this is John, one of the owners. John, meet Paul's sister, Heather. She's flown in from the UK for Christmas."

"Long flight for you," he said, reaching out a sinewy tanned arm and shaking her hand.

"Endless," she agreed. "But nice to arrive for summer." She tilted her head to one side. "Doesn't sound as though you're from around here, either?"

John's accent is straight out of California. Even so, I was surprised she'd picked it from only four words.

His startling blue eyes widened as his brows rose. "That was fast," he drawled, and the way he said 'fasst' was absolutely different from my Kiwi 'farst'. "Monterey Bay," he added.

"Actress in a past life," Heather said in explanation. "I picked up various accents for roles."

"Movies or stage?" I asked. Why hadn't Paul dropped that interesting snippet instead of describing her as childless and widowed and in need of cheering up?

"Stage and TV, but nothing too bigtime." She lifted both hands in a self-deprecating gesture.

Erik chose that moment to carry in a big flat basket of decadent looking muffins. He slid it under the glass-topped counter, and both Heather and I bent forward to peer at them.

Erik is something of a mystery. He's Erik Jacobsen, and he's from the Midwest. He calls John 'Jawn'. Everyone presumed the two Americans were father and son when they first arrived in the district, and then, as we got to know them better, maybe stepfather and son with their differing surnames. Or were they a gay couple? They made no effort to confirm or deny anything at all, and were very good at deflecting questions. Almost made a game of it.

Erik has a shock of short, frosty white hair in contrast to John's long streaky blond mane, but if you ignore the old-man hair, the face below it is virtually unlined. His eyes and brows are as black as his hair is white, and those eyes had fixed on Heather as though she was a tall drink of icy cold water in the burning hot desert. "Strawberry and white chocolate," he said, with a brief nod at the muffins. His gaze returned immediately to Heather.

I watched as she looked up at him. You could practically see the 'zing' of attraction sparking between them.

He turned away after a couple of electric seconds and called over his shoulder, "Debs, can you keep half an eye on things out here?" and without waiting for an answer he rounded the end of the counter and led us to one of the tables. He pulled out a chair, nodding for Heather to sit.

I glanced at Paul. He seemed oblivious to their attraction, but I caught the expression on John's face, and it was a mixture of 'you're kidding me' and 'go for it'. John and Erik are definitely not gay, by the way. Nor are they stepfather and son.

3

MARGARET'S MAKEOVER

WE ALL SAT – Erik next to Heather – and decided what we wanted to eat. Bacon and eggs for Paul, a ham and mushroom omelet for me, eggs Benedict for Heather.

"Earl Grey?" she suggested when Erik asked her what she wanted to drink.

I opted for coffee, and John shot away to pass the orders on.

"How long are you here for?" Erik asked, turning in his chair so Heather became the sole focus of his attention.

She blinked a couple of times. I won't say she was making eyes at him exactly, but there were definitely fluttering eyelashes. Maybe it was the bright sun. "Initially, six weeks. I might extend that if Paul can put up with me for a while longer." She tilted her head to the cloudless sky and closed her eyes like a basking cat. "I don't much fancy going back to an English winter if this is what's on offer."

Erik's dark eyes roved over her pretty features while she couldn't see him. It was almost as though he was memorizing her face. He didn't look away until John returned with a cup and saucer, and a teapot balanced on five side-plates. Erik set the cup and saucer and teapot in front of her and dealt the plates around the table like playing cards. It seemed they were joining us. Then John dived back behind the counter and emerged with knives and forks for Heather and Paul and me, and five of the strawberry and white chocolate muffins on a small tray.

"Oh, not muffins as well," I said, reaching out for one anyway, and then dropping it on my plate when I found it was still pretty warm. I sucked my tingling fingers for a few seconds, casting around for something to distract the others from my greediness. "Do either of you know a man called Beefy Haldane?" I asked.

Erik and John turned to me as though I was a puppet-master and had their heads on strings. Paul sucked air through his teeth, plainly not pleased I'd mentioned Beefy after he'd warned me off.

"Maybe," John said.

"Not well," Erik added.

At that moment another customer walked into the sunny courtyard. Manny and Dan immediately started barking, and the woman clutched her small white poodle more tightly against her large white breasts. Her neckline was pretty daring for someone who looked well past sixty.

John's two German Shepherds joined in from behind the

high fence, and a cacophony of growls and barks rent the air for a few moments.

"QUIET, BOYS!" I yelled at the spaniels, which was totally ineffective.

John gave a shrill whistle and the shepherds stopped dead. So did Manny and Dan. Only the poodle continued its high-pitched yapping.

"Margaret!" Paul exclaimed, rising to his feet. And sure enough, behind the gaping neckline and below the far-from-natural blonde hair it was Margaret Alsop, wife of Tom Alsop of A-One Autos and sister of Isobel Crombie whom Paul and I had found dead in Saint Agatha's church.

On the occasion of her sister's funeral Margaret had worn a very smart black suit, a small feathery hat perched on her silver curls, and a subdued but expensive selection of jewelry. This new version came as something of a shock.

Paul reached out, perhaps to pat her arm, and found the poodle in the way. The little dog was obviously upset and lunged at him, growling and snapping with its sharp white teeth. "Are you keeping well?" he asked, withdrawing his hand to a safer distance. "May I call by and see if there's any help the church can offer after all your work on the flower roster?"

"Things are settling," she said. "I had to sell the house, of course."

Understatement! Forced mortgagee sale by the bank or whoever Tom had borrowed all the money off for the overblown mansion in Sandalwood Grove. The Alsops had looked as though they were living the good life but suddenly he was in jail awaiting trial and inevitable conviction, given the evidence, and Margaret was out on her ear.

Paul nodded in his best understanding vicarish way. I'd gone spying in Sandalwood Grove soon after Margaret's unmarried sister had been murdered. They'd needed a dog-sitter for Isobel's two little Bichons while they swanned off on a tropical cruise. Paul had suggested me because I happened to be pinning a message on the community notice board right at that instant, offering just such a service.

"Where are you living now?" he asked.

She cuddled the little dog more securely against her big bosom. "In the old beach cottage at The Point. Our parents left it to Isobel and me jointly, so until the legal niceties are sorted out I thought it best to move in and keep an eye on things."

"And when things are finalized?" John interrupted. "Will you sell it?"

She looked surprised to be asked that by a virtual stranger. She blinked, and her mouth sagged open. "Ummm...?"

"There's a good surf break along that stretch of beach," he continued. "I asked Isobel to give me first right of refusal if she ever considered leaving."

Margaret patted the little dog and sighed. "Too early to think about it yet. Lord Drizzle's farm manager has been asking, too."

"Denny McKenzie?"

I caught the flash of annoyance that crossed John's face, but it was gone in a nanosecond. I'll bet he's a good poker player.

"He has a daughter getting married soon and thought it would be ideal for the newlyweds," Margaret said, dropping a kiss on the poodle's questing nose.

"When and if," John drawled, standing. "Can I show you to a table?"

She shook her head. "I just popped in to get something to eat while I'm out for a drive. Something savory I can share with Pierre," she added, looking down at her fluffy friend again.

Erik's eyebrows jumped. "Cheese and bacon croissant? Too good for a dawg, though."

"I'll get it," John said. He returned a few seconds later, croissant in one of the Burkeville Bar and Café's distinctive green-printed bags, and something else in another one. "Lamb-shank bone," he said. "Much better for him. On the house," he added, as Margaret tried to juggle both poodle and purse. "Remember I'm interested in the cottage if it goes up for sale."

She nodded her thanks and gave the spaniels a wide berth as she departed. I heard her shoes crunch over the gravel and then the car door being opened and slammed.

Huh! No electronic beeping. She must be getting around in Isobel's ancient Mini.

Erik grinned at John. "Pretty slick. Are you serious about that place on The Point or just fishing for info?"

"Serious for sure. Not in its current state though."

On the evening of Isobel's death John had scared me witless, striding up from the beach in a pair of wet board-shorts, clutching his surfboard under one arm, and looking as though he owned the place. Once he saw the fingerprint powder all around the lock and handle of the door he'd been very kind to me though. Sat me down with a hot drink and kept me company for a while, and I can confirm it was plenty distracting sitting opposite a man in such fine shape. His shorts were hidden below the table. He could almost have been naked. My naughty mind decided he was and enjoyed him even more.

"So," Erik said, black eyes fixing on mine. "Back to Beefy Haldane. Yes, we know of him, but how the heck do you?"

"I've never met him," I said, adopting my most innocent expression. "But Paul has. He broke into the Totara Flat church and drank the communion wine."

Paul looked total daggers at me. "Leave it, Merry. I told you he was a nasty piece of work."

"Cork's out of the bottle now," John said. "What's the rest of the story?"

When Paul didn't respond, I started to explain about going out to the garage to remove Graham's bag of golf clubs from the Mercedes so we could fit Heather's luggage in. And finding instead the huge chunk of beef with the notice on top aimed at Beefy Haldane. "DS Bruce Carver thought it prob-ably happened in the parking lot behind Graham's office because how could anyone get something like that past Manny and Dan at home?"

"And how is the good DS these days," John asked with an edge to his voice. "Still acting like he's God's gift to the district?"

Erik leaned closer to Heather. "He's thin and slippery is our DS Carver. Not the nicest cop you've ever met."

"I think he has a horrible job, generally dealing with awful people," I said in his defense. "Marion Wick is very pleasant." I aimed that at John to see how he'd react, and was annoyed to get only a vague nod.

Paul finally gave in and started to describe the scene at the church. The broken door, the haze of pot fumes, the shooting at the rafters. "He was drunk, and high, and way out of control. I was pleased when he staggered out and roared off."

"Sounds like he's got someone riled up from that message," Erik said. "Which direction did he go?"

"Mason's Ridge, or that's where he claimed he was heading. He could have gone anywhere. Just took off into open countryside on his big dirt bike."

I broke off a piece my muffin and ate it. My omelet seemed to be taking a while, although if Erik and John were both at our table, who was doing the cooking?

Erik gave John a somehow significant look. A twitch of an eyebrow, a slight lift of his chin. "Worth a look?"

John rubbed his nose. "Yeah."

"We could take a passenger," Erik said.

John looked at Heather but replied to Erik. "Yeah."

Something prickled between my shoulder blades. What were they really saying? A passenger to where?

Any further conversation was halted as the flame-haired waitress bustled over with Paul's bacon and eggs and my omelet.

"Thanks Debs," Erik said, pushing his chair back. "I'll get the last one." He returned a few seconds later with Heather's eggs Benedict and laid the plate before her like a gift.

She inspected the generous portion and glanced up at him, shaking her head. "It looks lovely, but I'll never manage the muffin as well."

"Breakfast *and* lunch," he reminded her. "We'll put the muffin in a bag for you and you can eat it when we get back."

"Back from where?" Paul asked.

I was wondering that too. Itching to know what the significant look between Erik and John meant.

Erik took a muffin from the tray, bit into it, and didn't answer until he'd swallowed. "Back from Mason's Ridge. John and I might take our tourist on a sightseeing trip in that direction. Show her a bit of the back-country. See what we can spot from the air."

"Now?" Paul and Heather asked in unison.

"When we've finished here."

"From the *air*?" I asked as the words sank in.

"I fly," Erik said, in much the same tone he might have said 'I walk' or 'I need a haircut'.

Heather's eyes widened. "I'd love to!"

Erik leaned toward her again and sent her a small but intimate smile. "You don't see much from the big jets. Too high. But we can give you a bird's-eye view in our whirlybird."

"You've got a chopper?" Paul demanded.

I hadn't known that either, but there were a number of small planes around the district, and I'd heard at least one helicopter. The farmers often have airstrips where the topdressing pilots can land and reload, even if they don't have a plane of their own. The surrounding hills are steep and getting sprays and fertilizer onto the land is often best done from the air.

John rubbed his nose. "Yeah – we fly in and out from Kirkpatrick's place. Keep her in an old barn there."

That was news to me. I thought I knew Erik and John quite well, but apparently not. How could they afford a helicopter? How had they paid for the Burkeville Bar and Café if it came to that? I'd never heard either of them groaning about mortgage repayments, and there's a nice-looking house on the property, too. Maybe they'd won a big lottery back in the States and escaped to the southern hemisphere with enough cash to start a whole new life? Maybe they were crooks and this was what they'd spent their ill-gotten gains on?

"Eat your omelet, Merry," John added. I must have been staring into space like a zombie as I reviewed possibilities.

"This is delicious," Heather said.

Erik reached for the teapot and poured her tea. "Ready for coffees yet?" he asked the rest of us.

"I'll go." John rose from his seat, casting an eye across to the two other occupied tables, and checking all was well before heading for the noisy coffee maker. He shuttled back and forth with a flat white for me, and long blacks for Paul, Erik and himself. I happen to know our vicar often prefers tea, but he tried the coffee, stirred quite a lot of sugar into it, and gulped it down without complaint.

But lucky Heather! Private sightseeing by helicopter. My blue eyes had probably turned a bit green. I speared a couple of slices of mushroom and tried not to look as though I minded, all the while cogitating about Margaret Alsop's transformation into an unlikely geriatric bombshell. With her husband Tom undoubtedly in jail for years ahead, was she trying to attract other men? Or finally looking like the woman she'd always wanted to be? She'd left it a bit late if so. Did men of sixty-plus find women of sixty-plus with big boobs on display and peroxided hair attractive? The only answer I came up with was 'possibly'. And where had the poodle come from? Why hadn't she taken over her sister's two little dogs, Itsy and Fluffy? They'd been absolute darlings and had started my whole pet-minding career. Yes, Lurline Lawrence at the Drizzle Bay Animal Shelter had been named in Isobel's will as the person who would find them their next home, but surely her own sister had precedence over butcher Bernie Karaka and his wife Aroha?

I turned to Paul as he set his coffee cup down. "Is Margaret still on the church flower roster?"

His gaze was fixed on Heather and Erik, and it was a very suspicious gaze. It looked as though he'd now well and truly spotted their mutual attraction. Protective brother? How would I feel if it was my sister making eyes at someone like Erik? A foreigner with secrets, and enough mysterious money to buy a helicopter? A handsome and assured man with a wolfish smile? Who was undoubtedly younger than his startling white hair indicated?

"Yes," Paul replied, but he was barely taking notice of me because he said to Erik, "Don't fly so close he can shoot you down."

Erik suddenly showed all his teeth. "I haven't lived this long without being careful. Heather will be in safe hands, never fear."

That was possibly what Paul was worried about!

"We'll do one high pass along the ridge," John said. "See if we can spot anything suspicious."

"Like concealed pot plantations, animals corralled where they shouldn't be," Erik inserted. "He may not even be there. Could be he was laying down a smokescreen when he mentioned Mason's Ridge."

"Possibly," Paul conceded. "But I think he was so high and so drunk he'd have had trouble blurting out anything but the truth."

Heather tilted her teacup and finished her tea. Her blonde hair shone in the sunshine and her mint-green and white striped T-shirt lit up her pale skin. She looked so fresh and pretty I wasn't surprised Erik was attracted.

"You want more tea?" he asked, already halfway out of his seat for her.

She shook her head. "Better not if you're serious about taking me flying."

"You know where Mason's Ridge is?" Paul asked, laying his knife and fork down on his empty plate.

Erik sat again, dug out his phone, and scrolled through a series of screens, turning it in Paul's direction when he found the one he wanted. "Maybe four miles from the coast, so four miles by air. Not far. We won't be long."

Paul narrowed his eyes and watched as Erik brought up an aerial shot of Burkeville and the main highway. I peered over his shoulder and Heather leaned even closer to Erik.

"Did you shoot this while you were flying?" I asked, fascinated by the way the muscles and tendons slid under his olive skin. No excess fat there, for sure!

He shook his head. "Taken from a lot higher than that. I have a buddy back home who works with satellite imaging, and he's sometimes willing to share special info." He scrolled across the countryside. "See – Kirkpatrick's farm. There's the barn where our big bird lives... and if we go further in this direction..." He moved on, and there were soon no roads visible. "So we're a couple of miles in now, and quite a lot higher. That's the *Pinus radiata* plantation you can see from the highway further north. That's Stanley Road. And here, at around four miles, is Mason's Ridge."

Paul shook his head as he focused on all the shades of green. The dips and hollows and up-thrust hills. "So you navigate with photographs instead of maps? How do you know what you're looking at?"

Erik showed all his teeth in a blazing grin as he tapped out a further instruction. Yellow forestry tracks and fire-breaks appeared over the vegetation. Then, in white, heights above sea level on some of the peaks, and occasional place names. Sure enough, Mason's Ridge showed clearly.

"How high is this shot from?" Paul asked.

In answer Erik pulled back and back until the coast showed green against the blue sea, and occasional clouds drifted by below. Then further still, until the whole of the North Island was visible, surrounded by ocean.

Paul and I goggled at each other. "From space," I said.

"Cool, huh?" Erik said, returning to the home screen as though he hadn't just shared a total miracle. "They're all shot from space these days. You look up any map and it asks if you want the satellite view."

"It does, doesn't it," Heather agreed. "But I've never seen all the empty pieces of countryside filled in with details like that."

Erik gave a secretive smile. "It's not what you know but *who* you know, sometimes."

The alarming files I'd discovered in the concealed office behind Isobel's garage swam back into my brain. I'd trans-ferred them to my Dropbox account, and just as well, because the office had been ransacked only hours later. I'd sent the files on to the Police once I'd been rescued and revived. Maybe I still had access to them? I could have another look and see exactly what they said about our hosts. Black Ops? Really?

Erik flexed his shoulders. "Jawn's right though – one high pass until we see how the land lies." He enclosed Heather's small hand in his, and rose.

Paul was definitely looking twitchy about having his sister stolen away.

I swallowed my last mouthful of omelet. "Shall we take the dogs for a walk on the beach?" I suggested.

"I'll have a quick word with Debs," John said, checking his watch. "Make sure she can cope without us for the next half hour." And a couple of minutes later the three of them roared away in John's black pickup truck.

———

PAUL UNTANGLED MANNY'S LEAD, and I gripped Dan's. We made it safely across the main highway and down a small flight of steps to the breezy beach, keeping to the strip of damp sand where it was easier to walk.

"We haven't paid for brunch yet," Paul said.

I laughed. "They've got a helicopter so they probably don't need our money." I pulled Dan away from investigating something that apparently smelled delicious to him – and smelled like dead fish to me. "Did you know about that?"

Paul shook his head. "Not a clue. They're a funny pair.

Run a good business. Affable and likeable, but even after all this time I know barely anything about them."

"Mmmm. They're secretive. I'd like to know more for sure. They come from different states. John told me he's from Southern California. I know Erik's not. 'Dawg' instead of 'darrg', which is how John says dog."

Paul rubbed his chin. "They're closer in age than I first thought," he said, kicking at a piece of driftwood. "Erik's hair is totally misleading. It's easy to presume he's twenty years older, and at first glance he's on the solid side, but it's all muscle. He's light on his feet. I knew guys like that in the army. Trained fighting machines. Hair-trigger reflexes. I'm pretty sure John was a SEAL, so what about Erik? Also something in the forces is my bet. And who's this 'buddy' who passes on the satellite shots with all that detail?"

I bent and picked up an iridescent paua shell, tilting it against the sun so the blues and greens and violets shone and sparkled. "You can find a lot online, but I've never seen maps with anything like that. So what are they doing here? Hiding?"

"It's a pretty public way to hide. Hiding in plain sight, but maybe." He cocked his head. "There they go."

Then I heard it, too. The unmistakable thump of rotors. We stopped and gazed in the direction of the noise and a few seconds later I caught sight of them. "Right – above the macrocarpa trees."

"Not a sound I'm fond of," Paul muttered, face contorted. I hated to think what he'd lived through in Afghanistan.

The little craft rose higher and flew straight for us, circling far enough out over the water that we weren't sand-blasted or drenched. Manny and Dan started a furious bark-off at the intruder, and I waved the paua shell at them. I think I saw Heather waving back to us. Then they peeled away, gained height, and headed inland.

"So what do you make of Margaret Alsop's new look?" I couldn't help asking once the noise had died away.

Even over the crashing of the waves I heard Paul draw a deep breath. "You have to remember she's had several big shocks in a row, Merry. First her sister, then her husband, then her house."

"And her fancy imported car," I added.

He looked across at me and nodded. "I think her very changed appearance is a result of all that."

"You're a very nice man, Paul McCreagh," I said, somewhat chastened.

"I agree she doesn't make an ideal blonde," he added, trying to hide a grin.

"But the neckline was *spectacular*," I chortled. "Just as well she had little Pierre to hide behind."

We walked on in the sunshine, occasionally pulling the dogs away from smelly treats in the long line of driftwood and seaweed at the high-tide line. After twenty minutes Manny's good ears heard the helicopter returning, so we changed direction and ambled back the way we'd come. Kirkpatrick's farm is only a few hundred yards up a side road, so we arrived right as they were pulling in to park the truck among the newly arrived lunch crowd.

Heather looked white as a ghost. Erik had his arm around her and she was leaning against his chest. Before Paul had any chance to object, she gasped, "It's terrible. He's dead!"

4

X MARKS THE SPOT

MY HAM and mushroom omelet made a sudden rush for freedom, and I clutched my ribs and swallowed hard to hold it down. Who was dead? Not John or Erik, so that left Beefy, or...?

"Come up to the house for a while," Erik said, leading the way along a path bordered with clumps of pink and cream miniature flaxes. He wasn't letting go of Heather. "Tie the dogs to the tree there. This won't take long."

"*Who's* dead?" Paul demanded.

"Back in half a minute," John called, striding through to check on things at the café.

"The late lamented Beefy, we're guessing," Erik snapped. "Does he have a better name than that?"

Paul looked nonplussed. "No idea."

By the time John had hurried back I'd secured Manny and Dan as instructed and Erik had unlocked their big cedar front door. He showed us into a room filled with sunlight and ocean views, and settled Heather on a big sofa, keeping his arm around her as though she'd fall over without his support. Maybe she would have. She was visibly trembling.

"All good," John reported on his return. "Debs is coping, and Warren's home from Auckland so she's got him helping out. I'll go back in a few minutes."

"In the meantime," Erik said, "it looks as though we have a case for DS Weasel."

"It was weird and horrible," Heather blurted. "There was a big driftwood tree that looked like an X. Someone had arranged him on it like a target."

"Fair enough description," John said, turning to Paul and me. "We were doing a bit of a loop, and a final pass along the beach to get Heather oriented to the local surroundings, and we couldn't miss him. Someone had heaved him up onto a huge piece of weathered driftwood, almost like they were showing him off. They meant him to be found."

"Not suicide?" Paul asked.

"Could you stretch your arms and legs out on a tree trunk after shooting yourself in the chest?" John asked.

Heather shuddered, and Erik drew her even closer.

John grimaced. "Definitely shot. Someone's sending a warning. Maybe using wild man Beefy as a signal to others to keep quiet."

"Almost like he was crucified," Heather added. "X marks the spot. I could barely look."

"I've got DS Carver's number here," I quavered, pulling

my phone and the iridescent paua shell from my small shoulder bag. I laid the shell on the side table and flicked through my contacts. "I had to call him about the cow in the car." I passed my phone across to John with a trembling hand. To my surprise he called direct instead of putting the number into his own phone.

"No – not Merry," he said when Bruce Carver answered. "I'm using her phone because I want to send you some photos from mine. Probably Beefy Haldane – the clown they left the notice for in her brother's car... Yep, sure." He waited a few seconds. I presumed he was being told the conversation would be recorded.

"Speaker?" he mouthed, peering at my screen, so I reached over and hit the right key. "Okayyyyy... we took Paul McCreagh's sister for a scenic flight this morning. Just to look at some of the district from the air. As far as Mason's Ridge." We all listened while DS Carver asked why.

"She's visiting from England. The three of them came here for brunch. It seemed like a friendly thing to do." He closed his eyes and dragged in a long, deep breath while DS Carver yakked on about not spreading the car break-in story any further afield. "Yep, but Merry was a bit rattled. She needed that car so she and McCreagh could collect the sister from the airport. Heather. Heather McCreagh."

"Heather Gregson," Heather said.

John raised an eyebrow. "She says Heather Gregson. Married name, maybe. *Anyway* the point of phoning you is to say that someone's dead. Shot, and arranged on a well-weathered tree on the beach down Drizzle Farm way. We're picking it's Beefy Haldane."

There was a short silence from the other end. I could picture DS Carver gnawing on his nasty fingernails. "What were you doing over Mason's Ridge?" he eventually demanded.

"Sightseeing. Showing off a bit of the local scenery. No law against that, is there?"

"Did you land?"

"No way, buddy. Never planned to. Flew around a bit longer and then spotted the body on the beach. He was hardly a sight to share close up with a woman. Bad enough from the air. Let me send a couple of shots through to you and you can get back to me about anything else later. We have a café to run here and the lunch crowd is arriving." He disconnected, and I pictured DS Carver's annoyance about not being the one to terminate the conversation. Not to mention being addressed as 'buddy'.

"That was a bit devious of you," I said. "Not saying why you headed to Mason's Ridge."

"Not his business to know," he said in a deceptively mild tone as he inspected what I presumed were the photos of Beefy. I leaned a little closer, hoping for a glimpse. Not a whole awful close-up, but perhaps just a whiff of the atmosphere?

"One," he said firmly. "And it's the highest one. You can't see a lot, which is probably for the best." He held out his phone very briefly. Sand, waves, a straggly white X in the center, and 'something' on top of it. He didn't let me look long enough to register any details. And I really didn't want to.

Heather buried her face against Erik's neck. "I've never been involved in anything like this," she murmured. "When Rob died..." She swallowed. "There was nothing sinister. I woke up one morning and found he was dead because his heart finally gave up. We'd known for years he was on borrowed time." She raised her head and looked across at Paul. "Sorry we didn't make you an uncle, but that was mostly why."

Her brother's expression was both thunderstruck and dismayed. "You knew but didn't tell us?" He sounded hurt and baffled.

"Rob's choice," she said. "He didn't want everyone tiptoeing around him on eggshells."

Paul gave a slow nod. "I still wish I'd known."

She heaved a gusty sigh. "But can you imagine how Mother would have carried on? Treating him like an invalid. Coddling me as though I was sixteen and helpless. She was bad enough when he died. "

"Mothers are allowed to fuss over their daughters when something that horrendous happens. You fussed over me when I first came back from Afghanistan."

"Yes, but you were..."

"I was *fine*," Paul insisted, obviously not wanting John and Erik to know about his PTSD. I couldn't help thinking they were the ideal people to talk with if he was right about their military backgrounds.

Erik shifted on the sofa, finally releasing Heather. "You gonna be okay?" he asked.

"I'll live." She stroked a hand down his forearm. "Thanks for looking after me."

Erik glanced at her fingers and laid his on top of them for a couple of seconds. "We'll do it again sometime soon. And to somewhere there's no chance of finding anyone dead. I guess the cops will want to talk to you. Just maybe don't tell them we might have been looking for Beefy."

"Lips are sealed," she said. "How would I know where we went or who we might have been checking on?" A mischievous smile transformed her serious face for a few seconds. "And brunch was lovely. Thank you."

We all rose. I collected Manny and Dan and we set off for my car while Erik and John returned to their customers.

Not even the boisterous dogs could cheer us up after something like that. They danced around, tugging on their leads because they knew another ride was following, and sniffed at Heather's bagged-up muffin until she raised it out of range. They both bounced up into the trunk of the Focus when I opened the hatch, wagging their tails and panting out big doggie grins, but even their joyful faces weren't enough to lift the mood.

We drove out onto the highway in somber silence. After a few minutes I put some music on, but whereas their cheerful howls on the way out had been a cause for hilarity, now the noise simply sounded painful. I switched the music off again.

"So," I said, because I thought we'd better talk about it, "What did Beefy do to deserve that? Who shot him? Why arrange him so grotesquely?"

No-one said anything for a while, and finally Paul cleared his throat. "It can't have been him who put the meat in the car. He wouldn't have left a notice threatening himself." He fell silent for a moment. "Although..." he added slowly, "I can't say I found him exactly sane. Maybe it *was* him and he was trying to deflect attention from himself somehow?"

"Funny way to do it," Heather scoffed. "He was obviously in danger though. Maybe he knew it. Do you think it was a warped cry for help?" She shuddered and wrapped her arms around herself despite the warm day.

"Do you want the air-con off?" I asked.

She shook her head. "No, I'm not cold. Probably shock."

"Do you think he lived out there?" I asked, tilting my head toward the forested hills.

I saw Paul's slow nod in the rear-view mirror. "He must have. Roddy's been gone a couple of months, and it would be about that long since Beefy broke into the Totara Flat church. They've probably set up camp in the trees. Unless there's an old forestry hut?"

"A bit close to civilization for that," I suggested. "Okay, let's suppose they have a hidden camp. How are they surviving?"

"Two crack shots," Paul muttered. "Shooting rabbits.

Trapping possums. He has that bike – some sort of farm bike, I guess. Good ground clearance. It would get him most places. He must leave the camp for fuel and other supplies, though. Maybe he goes further north for those?"

"How many guns does he have?" I asked.

Paul shook his head. "Too many. Even one would be too many, and I know he had the rifle he was shooting at the church rafters with. He was talking about buying more, and no doubt Roddy has others. They might have quite an impressive arsenal between them."

"All the district needs," I said, pressing my lips together.

He leaned forward. "Roddy claimed they were going to hunt and sell wild venison and pork."

"Which could be all above board," I said. "Although surely meat has to be certified safe by some sort of authority if it's for sale. Do you think the Police know about that?"

"I daresay," he said gloomily. "If they're hot on the trail of the rustling they'll be following all sorts of leads."

I glanced sideways at him. He was looking at Heather with concern.

"I'm wondering whether they transport it out or if they have a contact who goes in and collects it," I added. "They couldn't do much on one bike. Or even two bikes."

"It seemed very steep countryside," Heather said. "Mountains compared to England's hills. Erik thought someone else might be flying in. Maybe dropping a big sling down to them. Taking it out that way, if they're really doing it."

We fell silent for a few minutes. The waves surged and

splashed out past the sea wall, and the spaniels gave occasional whines to remind us they were there.

"It's very peculiar all round," Heather announced after more thought. "Merry – you said the detective thought the leg of beef must have happened while your brother's Mercedes was parked where he worked."

"Probably on Friday, because he flew to Australia on Saturday. I can't believe he wouldn't have smelled it if it had been any earlier than that."

"It's an expensive car. It wouldn't be easy to unlock."

I eased my foot off the accelerator of my Focus. On a fine day it's far too tempting to whizz along over the speed limit. "Graham's smart-key is always with him. He's the most orderly person you can imagine. No-one could take it without him knowing. There's a spare hanging up out of sight in one of our kitchen cupboards. That's what I used to open it with. If anyone had tried to force the lock, the alarm would have been tripped for sure."

"How public is the parking area?" she asked. "Who could have seen it happening?"

It didn't take long to think about that. "Probably nobody. The parking lot is behind the law offices. Various people use it. I haven't driven in there very often because there's plenty of room out in the street. I know there's a huge sycamore tree. Graham always parks opposite that so the birds can't poop on his car from the branches. And he always reverses into his space so he's facing out for a fast getaway." I couldn't hold in a puff of mirth. "If you'd met my brother you'd know how absurd that is."

I braked slightly to stay further back from a small dark green truck we were catching up to. The scent of animal dung was getting too strong, so I had a play with the car's ventilation. "Anyone upstairs would need to be right beside the window and looking straight down to see a person tampering with the trunk of the Mercedes. It's a good point."

Paul leaned forward again. "Carver has no doubt already asked him things like that."

"Well, maybe," I said. "But Graham's not home until later tonight, so he might be saving some of his questions for tomorrow. I hope my poor brother enjoys his double-strong cologne."

Paul grunted. "Warning you here, sis. He's always swamped with it. Take a hankie when he wants to see you. I'll bet he gets you sneezing."

I thought about that for a while. As Graham's friend wouldn't be dropping him off until after eight I could ask Paul and Heather home for a meal without having to contend with my darling boring brother's company. Nothing ventured, nothing gained. "Would you two like dinner with me? It won't be fancy, but I can rustle up some pasta and a salad?"

"And I can bring my muffin," Heather said. "Erik put it in a bag for me."

Ah – the elephant in the car had finally been mentioned.

I was sure Paul must be bursting with questions, and here was his opportunity.

"Speaking of Erik," he began.

"Don't start," Heather said with equal determination. "I'm a free agent, Paul-James. I haven't looked at another man since Rob died. If I want to look at one now, that's entirely my business."

"As long as it's only a holiday thing..."

Well, that seemed a bit much. It was her life, after all. Or did Paul have more info about Erik than he'd let on?

"What have you got against him?" Heather needled. "What do you know?"

I decided to listen along and not interrupt. Being a fly on the wall sometimes brings very interesting morsels to light.

Paul cleared his throat. I've noticed he does that when his next words are going to be significant. "What do I *know*? Not enough. Hardly anything at all, and that's the trouble. Erik and John arrived in the district about eighteen months ago. All of a sudden the Burkeville had new owners, and I hadn't heard a word about it being for sale, or that Paddy O'Donovan was thinking of retiring."

So much for listening along and not interrupting because I couldn't help inserting, "Paddy did say quite often he wanted to take a trip back to Ireland." I caught Paul's annoyed expression in the rear view mirror and returned my attention to the road.

"What about the planning, and the boasting, and all the little details Paddy was so fond of sharing?" he demanded.

"That man told everyone everything, but not a whisper about leaving. Not a hint. He was just gone and they'd taken over. Don't get me wrong – I like them well enough, but I know *nothing* about them. I didn't know they had a helicopter until today. That's a fairly significant detail. Where did they get the money from?"

"Shall I ask?" Heather said in an over-sweet tone.

"Good luck with that. They act perfectly open and friendly but they never actually share anything about themselves. I'm picking they both have military backgrounds."

"They've got the bodies for it," Heather agreed.

Paul practically snorted. "And I'm *also* picking they were into something a bit hush-hush."

OMG – had I ever let Paul know about their possible Black Ops work? I wracked my brains. I remembered phoning DS Carver from outside Saint Agatha's the evening Paul and I had had dinner together at the Burkeville Bar a few days after poor Isobel Crombie was murdered. I'd definitely mentioned finding strange files about car thefts and probably Black Ops in the secret office behind her garage. But had I ever linked John and Erik to the latter in Paul's hearing? Surely not. He'd have been all over me with questions if I had.

"Maybe they've taken early retirement from something a bit dangerous?" I suggested. "They could have got tied up with a big court case and been put into witness protection or something?"

"And come halfway around the world to hide," Heather said.

"They don't look like the hiding sort to me," Paul scoffed. "I'm sticking with my military theory. It takes one to know one."

Mmmm... he might be closer than he expected!

"Anyway – dinner?" I offered again. "In fact, Heather, would you like to come home with me for the afternoon? You can have another doze in the sunroom and sleep off some more of your jet lag if you like. Paul can join us later because he's no doubt got things to do."

"The Young Housewives Group," he said. "Arranging holiday activities for the children."

She sent me a smile. "I don't want to hold up your work, but I wasn't much looking forward to an afternoon on my own. Not with *that* to think about now."

"Thanks Merry," Paul said. "I'll bring a bottle. And I'll walk so there's no worry about driving home after a drink or two." He poked Heather on the shoulder. "Your shoes okay for walking?"

She grabbed his finger and tugged it. "You haven't grown out of doing that, I see."

"Ow," he said. "Your fingernails are too long."

"Now, now, children," I couldn't resist saying.

"Comfy enough sandals," Heather said, letting go of his finger. "But maybe I'll collect a cardi when we drop you off, Paul. I've still got the shakes a bit."

He gave her shoulder an affectionate pat before he

leaned back in his seat again. "Horrible start to your holiday. Not that anyone could have predicted that would happen."

"I wonder how it's going to finish..." she mused, staring out at the summer countryside.

Was she talking about finding the murderer or seeing more of Erik? Both were going to give me plenty to think about.

5

HEATHER AT HOME

I MADE a pot of Earl Grey and carried it through to the sunroom when we reached home. Heather curled up on the divan and I flopped down in the old cane chair Dad had been fond of.

"Don't let me hold you up from your work," she said.

"No worries. I keep my own hours." I gave the teapot a stir and let it sit a while longer. "I have something quite fun on the go right now. I've worked for this lady in the past. Elaine. She's kind of a modern day Beatrix Potter. She writes lovely stories for children about birds and animals, but she's badly dyslexic. A bit of a challenge to sort out sometimes."

"Spelling and punctuation?" Heather asked.

"And grammar that sometimes needs a helping hand." I poured her tea. "But it's so worth it. The finished results are gorgeous, because she does her own little watercolor paintings to go with them."

"You weren't joking about Beatrix Potter then?"

I shook my head. "Her hedgehogs are avoiding motor-bikes and fire engines, and there are no squirrels because we don't have them here in New Zealand, but there's Kewa the kiwi and Kerry the kereru."

Heather looked blank at that. "Our native wood pigeon," I added. "If Paul takes us walking in the bush we might see some. In fact, keep your eyes skinned for big birds sitting on the power lines. If they're getting on for chicken size but with really small heads and mostly dark green with a big white bib, that's them."

"Really small heads? Do they have big enough brains?"

I set her tea down beside her. "Shame on you, dissing our wildlife. Yes, I think they do. They never come down to ground level so they don't get run over, although I've heard they occasionally slam into car windscreens because they're slow to get up to speed after taking off out of trees."

She dropped a sugar cube into her tea. "There were prob-ably hundreds of them below us in all those pines."

"I don't think there'd be anything in a pine forest for them to eat. They need the native berries and buds."

And just like that she dissolved into tears as the fright of seeing the body on the big white X slammed back at her.

"Sorry," she sobbed, hiding her eyes. "It's hit me again. Oh, this is so stupid."

I galloped off to the bathroom and found a box of tissues for her. "Not stupid at all. Your circadian rhythms will still be out of whack and you had a heck of a fright.

That little glimpse John gave me on his phone was bad enough."

"How could someone do that to another person?" she said between sobs.

I picked up my cup. "I daresay Paul saw worse in Afghanistan. And I know Beefy Haldane lived through absolute hell there. I did a bit of research after Paul first mentioned him – not that I told him that. Beefy got hooked up with an orphanage, and used to go back and help out in his time off. Maybe it made him feel he was there for the right reasons. He'd bonded with one of the little boys and wanted to somehow adopt him, or at least sponsor him."

Heather nodded, and sniffed into her tissue.

"A terrorist with a grudge followed him to the orphanage and stormed the school."

"No!"

"Killed everyone, or so they thought. Beefy was left for dead and they found later that the little boy had been kidnapped. Converted to their cause, with pretty horrible results. A tiny terrorist. A group of UN soldiers found Beefy more dead than alive and he came home a total mess – badly injured and hooked on pain meds." I took a sip of my tea. "I can't imagine how he'd ever live a normal life after that."

"I'm going to pretend," Heather said, "he was shot fast and didn't know anything further. And being put on the cross happened after he was dead."

"Good idea," I agreed. "I can't imagine it's possible to make a live person lie down like that. I doubt there were many people there. It looked totally deserted from the quick glimpse of the photo I had."

"Just empty beach," Heather said. "No-one visible for miles. Only sheep and cows."

I set my cup down. "I'd love to know who killed him, and why – seeing the leg of beef turned up in our garage. It's hard not to be curious after something like that." I looked at her more closely. "Did Paul tell you much about a guy called Roddy?"

She shook her head. "Something about him having guns?"

"Yes – he went bush with Beefy."

"And by that you mean...?"

"Took off out into the wild. Don't you say 'went bush' in England?"

She shook her head.

Ah. How did I explain Roddy to Heather without letting slip he'd followed her brother from Afghanistan to New Zealand and declared everlasting love. Or lust. Or some sort of other totally misguided emotion? And been overheard by Isobel Crombie, who may or may not have told her sister before she was murdered in Paul's church? Heather would know about the murder, of course. It was unlikely Paul could have kept that a secret from her.

"Roddy and Beefy went hunting together," I said. "So maybe Beefy was still hooked on drugs and went berserk? And was killed because he couldn't be subdued."

Heather grimaced. "By Roddy? So he'd be the murderer?"

I took another sip of tea. "If that's what really happened. But it might not have been. Beefy was a handsome hunk before he got so unkempt. I could picture him being popular with women."

"You?" Heather asked, sleepy eyes now wide awake. Had she been wondering about any attraction between Paul and me?

I shook my head. "It's one thing to find a man handsome, but it's quite another to do anything about it! I'll show you what Beefy looked like in his better days."

I rose and retrieved my laptop from my office, found some photos of him I'd tracked down, and passed it across to her.

"Mmm," she said. "Strong face. Good eyes. I could go for that."

I grinned at her candor. "Erik's sort of build," I said.

She raised her eyebrows but said nothing.

"So maybe Beefy got involved with a lady or two," I suggested. "Broke their hearts. And someone decided he needed teaching a lesson."

"But not a woman," she said. "Not to do that."

"Wife of someone who hunts? Wife of a farmer who could grab a gun? I'm considering all possibilities here."

Heather rubbed her chin. "But how would a woman get him alone on the beach? And arrange the tree thing?"

"If he was keen on her, getting him alone on the beach wouldn't be hard."

She pressed her lips together, trying to stifle a laugh, I suspected. "Maybe, but the whole scenario's pretty odd."

"Considering the woman theory further, maybe she shot him somewhere else and a brother or husband discovered what she'd done and arranged the disposal side of things?"

"Not buying it," Heather said. "If you'd seen it, you wouldn't think that. You wouldn't throw a body in the trunk of a car, drive it across the countryside, heave it out on the beach in the open, and arrange it on a tree."

We both got the giggles at that. "No," I conceded. "Probably not."

"Be better to tip it down a gully," she added. "Plenty of lonely winding roads and steep countryside here from what I could see from the air."

I closed the laptop. "An aggrieved husband makes more sense as a murderer than a spurned woman. I can picture them wanting to flatten him if they found he'd seduced their wife or daughter."

"But again," Heather said, "How did they get him out there? Either they had to shoot him close to where we saw him, or they had to transport the body somehow."

I swallowed the last of my tea. "So we come back to drug-dealing or rustling and skulking around in lonely places. They're the things that make the most sense."

She nodded slowly and raised her cup for another sip.

I settled further back into Dad's old chair. "I think I know why he's called Beefy. He's Bernard Edward Ewan Forrester Haldane."

She stopped abruptly before drinking. "You're kidding me. That's a big name for a poor little baby. Huh – B.E.E.F. Yes, I suppose some cruel schoolboy thought it made a good nickname."

"So let's say Beefy is something to do with the rustling from Jim Drizzle's farm that Bruce Carver doesn't want us talking about. Beefy might have been trying to make deals on the side to finance his drug and alcohol habit if he knew about all those cannabis plants on Mason's Ridge."

"Drugs *and* alcohol?" Heather asked.

I shrugged. "Going by what Paul told me."

She set her cup down on its saucer and wrapped her arms over her chest.

"Are you cold?" I asked.

She shook her head. "A bit spooked."

I reached across and snagged the corner of the big old hand-crocheted rug that had lived on the back of the other cane chair since our mother died. Maybe Graham and I left it there in case she magically reappeared and wanted it again. Heather didn't need to know that. "Throw this over your legs. If you want to doze off I'll wake you in plenty of time for dinner."

"Erik might call," she said, avoiding my eyes.

Might he indeed! I tried to look not the least bit interested. "Your phone will wake you then. I'm popping down to the Mini-mart for a couple of things. I'll lock the back door.

The dogs will bark plenty if anyone turns up while I'm gone."

I collected the cups and saucers and took them out to the kitchen, poking them into spaces in the dishwasher, and thinking hard. How could I find out more about the rustling on Drizzle Farm? I was expecting to receive Jim's memoirs to knock into shape sooner or later, so maybe that was my starting point? And if I was taking the car to carry the groceries I could tootle ten minutes down Drizzle Bay Road and see if he was home (likely) and up for a chat (possible) and willing to talk about the rustling (somewhat less likely).

I always think it's worth striking while the iron is hot, and I didn't have much to lose, so off I went. First to the Mini-mart for wavy lasagne noodles and a couple more cans of tomatoes because once I checked the cupboards I found my offer to provide pasta and salad wasn't backed up by much in the way of ingredients. They had lovely fat shiny capsicums in the produce department, and really good avocados, too. Would Paul and Heather like avocados? Yes, everyone in the world seems to like them these days. I bought a couple so we could have half each for a starter.

Starters put me in mind of desserts, of course. Okay, yes, we'd had those delicious white chocolate and strawberry muffins at the Burkeville, but brunch was now hours behind us. A quick visit to Iona Coppington's café was called for, and what did I find? Darling little Christmas pudding cupcakes with marzipan icing that wouldn't melt like frosting. Should

I ask her to keep three aside for me, or should I risk a trip to Drizzle Farm with them?

I pointed into the glass-fronted display case. "Will those be safe in the car for a while?"

Iona wiped her hands on her big white apron and blew a feathery wisp of hair out of her eyes. "Depends if you have the spaniels in there." She knew their greedy ways from past disasters.

"No, Iona. They're at home keeping Paul McCreagh's sister company." Not quite a lie, and it seemed as good a way as any to give Heather a mention. "She's here for Christmas, and for a few weeks to follow. You don't want any help with Christmas baking for a while, do you? She was going to enter The Great British Bake-off last year."

Iona tilted her head on one side. She looks just like one of those white Australian cockatoos when she does that – inquisitive black eyes, beaky nose, fat little face and ruffled white feathery hair. I wouldn't be surprised to see a crest of Sulphur-yellow plumes zoom up on top of her head and hear a few squawks of indignation issue forth if something really riled her.

"Why didn't she, then?"

I worried at my bottom lip. It wasn't really my story to tell; I shouldn't have mentioned her. "Her husband died," I said. "I probably shouldn't have told you. Not my business."

"Bring her along for coffee tomorrow," Iona said. "I could certainly do with an extra pair of capable hands for a week or so. I'll sound her out. See if she's anything more than a keen amateur." She blew the hair out of her eyes again. "And the Christmas pud balls will travel fine. Solid as little rocks."

Well, that didn't sound entirely appetizing! Then again, Iona cooked like a goddess so I probably had nothing to worry about. "Right – three of those." A picture of Graham flashed into my mind. He'd be home later tonight, travel weary, worried about the state of his car, and missing his dogs. "No, better make that four."

Iona smiled as she picked them up with her tongs and placed them reverently in a small white cardboard box. "There's a surprise inside some of them," she said with a twinkle in her birdy eyes. "I hope you get at least one of the surprise ones."

I handed over a twenty dollar note and didn't get as much change as I expected. They'd better be special for that.

I put the box on the floor to keep it out of the sunshine and set off for Drizzle Farm. The pohutukawa trees behind Saint Agatha's were ablaze with scarlet tassel flowers, and I spotted others as I drove along Drizzle Bay Road. Lisa had curled some bright green tinsel around and around the top railing of the fence outside the vet clinic. Talk about spooking the horses! I spotted several Christmas wreaths on doors, and the agricultural pump place had really gone for broke with little twinkling lights back under the eaves so they showed up quite well, even on a bright sunny day like this.

I felt a bit guilty I hadn't made more of an effort. Our front door boasted its usual wreath but that was the sum total of my decorations. Graham is not a frivolous person. There's no chance he'd ever consider climbing onto the roof and wiring a light-up Santa to the chimney. Or standing illuminated reindeer in the front garden.

But Graham wouldn't be home for hours yet, and I knew our mother's old suitcase of Christmas decorations was still stowed on top of the spare bedroom wardrobe. Surely it wouldn't take long to do a bit of winding and festooning on the lower branches of the loquat tree by our front boundary before he got home? Poor old loquat tree – it was very obliging, living on in the salty spray when people expressed doubt and surprise it could survive at all, not to mention that it produced annual crops of little yellow fruit our mother had never bothered to make jelly from. It had branches I could reach from a couple of steps up the ladder, and they'd be too high for dogs and small children to get at. I could have quite a bit of fun with it before Graham returned.

Full of inspiration and enthusiasm, I arrived at Drizzle Farm to find the brick gateposts and the black lanterns on top of them looking terribly tasteless and amazingly festive. Someone – presumably young Alex – had really gone to town with the tinsel and baubles and bright foil streamers.

There was no one in sight so I turned in between the garish gateposts and smirked my way up the long farm driveway. Bright welding sparks were visible in one of the barns before I reached the house, and I thought I recognized those corduroy trousers. I pulled off to the side and waited for the work to stop.

It took less than ten seconds for the brilliant sparking to die away and Lord Jim Drizzle came stumping out, pushing the visor of his old black welding helmet up and giving me a cheery wave as I hopped out of the Focus.

"Little Merry!" he exclaimed with apparent pleasure. "Just doing some strengthening on one of the trailers. Can't have the tow-bar giving away."

Indeed! "Good on you, Uncle Jim." (If it was good enough for him to keep using my childhood name then it seemed fair enough I kept up the Uncle Jim pretense, even though he isn't.) "Are we on our own?" I asked. "I wanted to sound you out about something a bit delicate. Or something DS Carver asked me to keep quiet about, anyway."

Jim pulled the welding helmet off and added a few more wrinkles to his already corrugated face as he frowned. "And that would be?"

"I understand there's been some rustling from the farm."

"How the...?" he asked, looking none too pleased.

"It's not going any further," I hastened to reassure him. "Has he been in touch with you recently?"

Jim shook his grizzled head. "Not in the last several days."

I leaned back against the car. Someone was still banging around inside the barn, so I dialed my volume down. "Expect a call, then. I found a quarter of a cow in the trunk of Graham's car. In the garage at home."

Jim's impressive eyebrows rose about half a mile.

"The hide was still on it," I added. "Black, so probably

Angus. I let the police know of course, and there were finger-print people swarming around in no time. DS Carver told me to keep it to myself because they're hot on the trail of some-one, but he did mention you'd had rustling problems recently. Have you had any Angus cattle go missing?"

Jim nodded, looking furious. "Another few gone last week."

"And have you heard of anyone called Beefy Haldane?"

That really got his eyebrows going, and he opened his mouth, presumably to swear, and then thought better of it in a lady's company. Am I a lady? Possibly, in his eyes, yes.

He didn't swear anyway, but he kind of clamped his whole face shut with annoyance for a few seconds. "Worked here for maybe a month, beginning of winter. My farm manager, Denny McKenzie, took him on and then couldn't get rid of him fast enough. He was only here for a few weeks. High as a kite most of the time, according to Denny. I don't mind giving people a chance if they're down on their luck, but if they soil their copybook then they're out on their ear."

I took a second or two to unravel all the clichés and then I said, "There was a notice on top of the cow which said 'Beefy Haldane better watch out'."

Jim pulled the corners of his mouth down. "Not entirely surprised. He was a soldier once but he seems to have fallen in with a bad lot and gone downhill."

"It's worse than that," I said. "He's dead."

Jim's jaw dropped, then he recovered, tossed the welding

helmet onto the grass, and angled his chin toward the big old farmhouse. "Cup of tea, eh?"

I trailed him inside and spilled the whole story as we drank our tea – the locked car, brunch at the Burkeville, and Erik's unexpected announcement he had a helicopter parked nearby and was willing to give Heather a scenic flight after Beefy Haldane was mentioned.

And what they'd found on the deserted beach.

"So," I concluded, "You can probably expect a call from Bruce Carver sometime pretty soon. I'm not meant to talk about it, but if it's your cow and Graham's car then I'm sure we both want to know more as soon as possible."

"I knew Haldane was still around the district," he said. "Last I heard he was doing some wetlands planting and maintenance for Perce Percy at Devon Downs. Perce knew he was pretty unhinged and had given him an abandoned shearer's cottage rent-free to keep him out of circulation. Hoped he might calm down a bit with somewhere to live and a job to keep him occupied."

I sipped the last of my tea. "So he wasn't living at Mason's Ridge?"

Jim shook his head.

"I'd heard he'd gone hunting with someone else and planned to sell venison and wild pork."

"Not up there," Jim said, pouring us both another cup and nudging the tin of cheese scones in my direction again. I certainly didn't need one, but Lady Zinnia Drizzle used to win most of the baking classes at the annual summer fair, so who was I to turn down such culinary treasure? Not just wonderfully sharp cheese, but delicious little 'pops' of something. Whole-seed mustard, maybe?

She wasn't visible to ask, but I could smell turpentine wafting from somewhere inside the big old house. These days Lady Zinnia paints exuberant florals in oils. Not the sort of thing Winston Bamber's classy gallery would ever exhibit, but she donates them to school fairs and other fund-raising events, and I'm sure they're hanging out there all over the place. Our father bought one a few years ago and it graced the wall of the spare bedroom for ages. And somehow never re-appeared when Graham and I had the room repainted after our parents died and it became his study.

"There was a bit of a 'situation' between old Perce and young Beefy," Jim added with noticeable reluctance. "As Perce is selling up, and Beefy's dead, it won't hurt to tell you." He looked down at the battle-scarred table top. "Beefy is the bastard son of either Perce or his wife. Wasn't brought up with them, but rumors were pretty rife years ago."

"Heavens to Betsy!" I exclaimed. I've possibly not said that before in my whole life, but it seemed a suitable comment on something so old-fashioned and odd. "He fought in Afghanistan, I gather. And ended up badly wounded and hooked on drugs."

"Perce is a snob," Jim said. "Always was. Married Maisie Hardacre back in the seventies and she was even worse. They built a huge house, threw parties you wouldn't believe. She brought money to the marriage, and they splashed it around like water for a while." He took another sip of his tea. "And then she disappeared mysteriously for a few months. No one knew for sure if the marriage was in trouble and she'd left him and was enticed back, or whether she went off to have a baby in secret. For sure it wasn't Perce's child if that's what happened or it would have been brought up at home with them."

"But if Perce got someone else pregnant the wife might have left in a huff?"

"Exactly," Jim said, nodding slowly. "Either way, when the boy turned up as a young man Perce was absolutely livid to find either he or she had spawned a loose-living, low-life druggie. I think there were only a couple of us knew," he added, "and you don't kick a mate when he's down. Not that he was ever such a great mate, but a near-enough neighbor, and the same generation, so..." He shrugged.

"So was Beefy on drugs from early on?" I asked. "Someone told me he probably got hooked on them after he was wounded in Afghanistan. He must have cleaned up his act to ever get into the Army?"

"Total disappointment," Jim said, which didn't quite confirm or deny anything. "They had no other children so it's the end of an era for Devon Downs. Probably end up under foreign ownership and get turned into yet another dairy farm," he added. His bristly eyebrows drew together in a fierce frown.

"Oh well, water under the bridge now." I swallowed the last mouthful of scone and rose reluctantly from the comfy old kitchen chair. "I need to get home. Your gateposts have inspired me," I teased as we walked out into the yard. "Graham's not back until after dark so I thought I'd jazz up the loquat tree out the front."

"That's Alex's work," Jim said, gazing across at the old green bus where orphaned Alex Hudson presumably still slept after his mother's tragic death from an inoperable brain tumor. "Good lad. Shaping up well."

Lord Drizzle often provided short-term farm jobs for foreign students keen to trade their labor for temporary accommodation and work experience. Alex was more than that – almost an extra grandson now from what I could see – and they were working on the Drizzle memoirs together. I looked forward to learning a lot more about my Dad's old friend in due course. And his motorcycle racing. My brain still boggled a bit at the thought of Jim hurtling around a track far too fast in slapdash safety gear, but that was life back then.

"I'm without Denny for a few days," he said, leaning an elbow on my car roof. "Bad situation for him. Wife being treated for cancer and their only daughter getting married and insisting they change the wedding to a resort in Fiji. I think they've hurried it up, in case. They flew out yesterday."

I pictured the sunshine and swaying palms. Maybe everyone barefoot on golden sand. "Sounds beautiful. But sad, of course, if the mother's so ill."

"Denny's hopping mad," Jim added. "They had everyone invited to a big local shebang mid-January. Caterers booked, deposits paid, and then the daughter put her foot down. Half the guests don't want to pay for airfares and accommodation in Fiji, or can't get enough leave from jobs at this time of year to make it worthwhile, and Denny feels it's far too much strain on Lorraine." He reached out and opened the car door for me. "Bad all round," he concluded. "I think the daughter hoped it would be a treat for her mother, but weddings are stressful at the best of times. And this isn't the best of times, by a long shot."

"Families," I agreed. "Not as bad as the Percy family, though. Anyway, I'll be in touch if I hear anything useful about Beefy Haldane."

I whizzed off home again, music too loud because it was that sort of day, and found a smart black pick-up truck parked outside in the street. It looked like John's, but what would he be doing here?

After lifting the box of Christmas pudding cupcakes with great care, and the big bag of groceries with rather less, I hurried inside. To my surprise I found not John but Erik, and he was looking right at home in the sunroom with Heather. She was curled up on the divan with the rug over her legs, much as I'd left her. He was sitting by her feet, rubbing a hand to and fro from her ankle to her knee in a slow, soothing caress.

6

DINNER FOR FOUR

HEATHER WAS whiter than winter snowdrops. She opened her eyes when she heard me enter the room, but then she scrunched them shut again for a few seconds.

Erik stood, like the gentleman he might be, and gave me a polite nod.

"You'll never guess what this foolish man did," Heather said through clenched teeth. "Went straight back to that body without anyone to help, and they might have *shot* at him."

I probably opened and shut my mouth like a goldfish a couple of time, because what can you say in reply to something like that? A few seconds later I found I'd grabbed a fistful of my watermelon-pink blouse and was pressing my hand down against my heart.

Too bad if I ended up with a patch of crumples.

The steady beat possibly calmed me a little, but it would

have made more sense to grab Erik's shirt and make sure he was the one still alive.

Yeah – not going to happen. He looked mega-alive. Cool and steady. As though he was thriving on the situation. He was soon sitting by Heather again and once more had a big hand curled around her ankle.

"You're okay?" I asked him.

He looked across at me with his unnerving dark eyes. "Never better." His mouth twitched at the corners and he took a deep breath because I saw his broad chest expand, which stretched his green Burkeville Bar polo shirt most decoratively. The man was solid muscle.

I let go of my blouse. "Why on earth did you do it?"

"Wanted to get lower. Couldn't take the risk when we had Heather with us."

She glared at him and huffed, "But you'd risk your own life!"

Now there were two anger spots blooming on her pale cheeks. I absolutely saw her point of view. From what she'd seen on the first flight, someone was up to huge amounts of no good down by the beach. Why would anyone go back for another look?

Erik shook his head. "Not so much of a risk."

"But they could have shot at your engine," she said.

He gave the slightest of grins. "Engine's up above me. If they'd hit that, the bullet would have gone straight through me and I wouldn't be worrying much."

"I might be," Heather snapped. Then she gave a very obvious swallow. "Really?"

I sagged down in Dad's big cane chair. "Why didn't you wait for DS Carver to swing into action? Or whoever it would be if they had to get someone else out there?"

Erik planted his other hand on his knee and sat there as solid and still as the First World War memorial in the main street of Drizzle Bay. "Striking while the iron was hot. I could get back there in a few minutes. No idea how long it would take for them to deploy someone from further away. Every minute means evidence can be hidden or destroyed."

"But hang on, why's that your business?" Would he admit he and John were somehow working in cahoots with the Police or one of the government departments? That word 'deploy' surely smacked of a military background.

"Concerned citizen," he said without blinking. "Had the means to lend a hand."

"Lend a *body*," Heather muttered. "Lucky you didn't."

By now I'd stopped being so shocked and had the story straighter. "So no-one actually shot at you? Did you see anyone?"

Erik took another slow breath before speaking. "No-one shot at me. I'm sure no-one was around. There's nowhere much to hide down there. I took a chance and went down pretty low." He waited a few seconds while Heather and I made disapproving noises like a pair of old grannies. And," he said, pausing and grimacing, "that's not Haldane on the tree."

"What?" we exclaimed in unison. "Who?" We must have sounded like one person in an echoing cave.

Erik shrugged. "Haldane's dark. Big beard. This guy had long hair, lighter brown, no beard to speak of. The downdraft swept his hair back and I got a decent look this time. Still dead though."

I sat up straighter, wondering if it was Roddy. I had no idea what *he* looked like of course. If he'd been a soldier until a few months ago, could he have long hair by now?

"Already sent Carver some much better shots," Erik added. "Hopefully good enough to ID him from. I needed to stay well back – far enough I didn't blow any of the evidence away."

"You'd better tell Paul," I said to Heather. And then realized I needed to get back to Jim Drizzle and let him know it wasn't Beefy before the story went any further. "Excuse me just a mo," I said, trotting off into the back yard and confessing to Lord Jim that I'd been barking up the wrong tree, so to speak. The spaniels galloped over and gave my legs a good sniff in case I'd been anywhere interesting since they'd last seen me. Could they smell Iona's café or the produce department of the Mini-mart? I gave each silky head a rub, and played with Manny's ears while Jim huffed and puffed on the other end of the line.

"So he's still out there somewhere, and maybe planning to steal more of my cattle," Jim said, sounding pretty peeved. "A good Angus bull can fetch close to three thousand dollars. I don't breed them for criminal scum to profit from."

That was pretty strong language from polite old Jim! "It might not be him doing it, of course," I soothed. "Could be someone else entirely. I'll pass on anything Bruce Carver tells me – not that I'm expecting a flood of confidences from that direction."

"Good girl, Merry. Thanks for letting me know anyway."

I gave the spaniels a final pat and shot back inside, glancing at my watch. No time to get the Christmas decorations onto the loquat tree right now – the promised lasagne took precedence. But first I returned to the sunroom, walking ever more slowly so I could listen as words like 'commercial' and 'frontwoman' and 'scenery' drifted out. I poked my head through the doorway. "Are you two okay? Like tea or coffee? Anything?"

It definitely wasn't my imagination; they were now sitting closer together. And looking like a pair of conspirators.

They shook their heads about drinks, and I mumbled something about making a start on dinner and went back to the kitchen.

A frontwoman for a commercial? Heather had let slip she used to be an actress, so what were they cooking up together? I couldn't hear their voices any longer, even though it was the quietest lasagne I'd ever made. Then there was a big burst of barking from the spaniels and Paul arrived – earlier than expected, but at least dinner was now well under way.

He brandished a bottle of Merlot. "You said pasta?" He sniffed, and then closed his eyes. The kitchen now smelled like somewhere in Tuscany or Umbria and seemed to meet with his approval because he opened them again and smiled. "Looking forward to this," he said.

"Don't get your hopes up too high," I warned him, taking the wine and setting it on the counter. "That looks ideal. Thank you."

"How is she now?"

A fond brother probably doesn't want to hear his sister has spent the last couple of hours with a hunk like Erik sitting at the foot of her bed and making affectionate advances to one of her legs. Or that he'd now moved closer and they definitely had their heads together about 'something'.

"She's had a nice rest," I said. That was certainly true. "She's in the sunroom with Erik, because he came by with some pretty interesting news."

Paul instantly lost his casual air, sucked in a quick breath, and squared his shoulders.

I waved him through, wondering how close Heather and Erik would now be. "I'll just set the table. Be there in a minute."

Or maybe I'd be there right away, because I could ask Erik to join us and perhaps learn more. The chances of him being available were slim, but you never knew unless you asked.

Heather was sitting on the divan with her feet on the floor. I wondered if she'd straightened up because she'd heard Paul arriving.

"How are you doing?" he asked, touching her shoulder.

She grimaced and shrugged. "Very strange day. Better now some time's gone by. I've stopped shaking anyway."

The two men shook hands. Paul looked tall and on edge. Erik seemed entirely relaxed.

"How about we go into the big front room?" I suggested. "More chairs. And who'd like a drink, because Paul's brought a nice bottle of Merlot."

"Lovely," Heather said, reaching out a hand to Erik.

As none of my guests had ever been into the big front room before, I led the way. "My mother's favorite room," I said, waving them to the chairs and sofas.

"I can see why," Heather said. "Great view."

Yes, it was. We needed more visitors to come and admire it, not that Graham was likely to change his mind any time soon about being sociable. Since our parents had died we'd had the front fence taken down and a new one built which ran from the corner of the house to the garage, and another from the front of the house to the side fence, effectively keeping the spaniels safely confined. They had the whole of the back yard to tear around in, and we gained the entire ocean to look at. Not a bad trade. Now only a band of easy-care miniature Peter Pan agapanthus marked the front boundary – currently covered in a nodding forest of knee-high blue flowers.

Across the road, big frothy waves lost their fight with gravity, tumbled over, and slid up the broad expanse of sand. Beyond them the sun-dappled sea stretched all the way to the horizon. In the near distance, Brett Royal's whale-watch charter boat ploughed its way back toward the dock. It was the view I'd grown up with, the beach I'd built sandcastles on, and where I adored walking the dogs.

"Anyway, sit," I said. "I'll get the glasses." Not wanting to miss anything I was back in a flash with four wine goblets, a dish of cashew nuts, and the bottle of Merlot balanced on a tray. I set it down and Paul reached for the bottle. No-one was speaking. Heather and Erik had seated themselves on a sofa. Paul had claimed one of the chairs. I perched on the other sofa, nobly depriving myself of the view. Who was going to break the ice?

It seemed it would be me. "Paul – Erik has some pretty shattering news."

Paul had just picked up the first glass, but he stopped before tilting the bottle. I saw his gaze slide from Heather to Erik.

"Nothing to do with me," she said. "And I'm still hopping mad about this. Erik flew straight back to that body after we left this morning."

"What does Roddy look like?" I demanded of Paul.

"Why?" Heather asked. So that answered the question of whether Paul had told his sister much about his inappropriate stalker. Plainly not.

Paul set the bottle down without pouring a drop. "Fair like Heather," he said, offering no further description.

"Not him then," Erik said, leaning back into the sofa. "When I went back on my own I did a pretty thorough recce. No-one around that I could see, so I –"

"Flew down really low!" Heather exclaimed. "Honestly, how stupid can you get?"

Erik didn't seem to mind her annoyance. Indeed, he grinned faintly, drew her hand down onto his thigh, and left his own on top of hers so she couldn't pull it away. I saw Paul's gaze follow their hands before he looked up at Erik's face again.

"Wasn't Haldane," Erik drawled. "Once the downdraft pushed his hair away, that was plain. Long, light brown hair. Skinny dude. Not Maori."

"Wasn't Roddy either, then," Paul said. "When I last saw him he had a buzz-cut from Afghan. No time for it to grow far in a few weeks."

Heather wound some of her hair around a finger and then let it go again. She glanced across at Paul with an enquiring frown.

"Someone I counseled over there. Came to New Zealand and teamed up with Beefy Haldane."

Well, that wasn't quite true, but it seemed it was the version Paul wanted his sister to know. Fair enough – we all have our embarrassing secrets. Paul's hopeful gay stalker now seemed to be well out of his way and it was probably best he remained there.

"So we know Haldane's still on the loose," Erik said, bringing us back to the point.

"And possibly living at Devon Downs, according to Jim Drizzle," I inserted.

Erik grimaced. "So maybe nowhere near Mason's Ridge

after all? Despite that warning in your brother's car, he hasn't come to any harm yet."

"Someone else has," I said glumly. I glanced across at Paul. "Yes, pour us all a drink – I think we need it."

"But to lighten the mood, we have something worth celebrating," Erik said. "We're expanding. Getting a seven-seater Squirrel AS355."

I must have looked really blank because he circled a finger in the air a few times, fixing me with his super-dark eyes and inviting me to guess.

"Helicopter?" I asked. "Another one?"

"Bigger one – for our new business."

Paul immediately brought the bottle of wine upright again. "What about the Burkeville? Are you selling it?"

Erik shook his head. "Nope – got it working well. Debs will take over as manager. She's doing ninety percent of the job already."

"So...?" I asked.

"Heli-tourism." He rubbed his hand over Heather's, to and fro in a soft caress. "Get folks to where they want to be a lot faster. Family trips some of the time. Flights over areas they'd never normally see. Set down somewhere great for a picnic –"

"Food from the Burkeville," Heather inserted.

"You got it! Maybe visit caves with pre-historic paintings, waterfalls no-one has access to, enjoy a swim somewhere pristine and unpolluted, whatever the best local features are. But way off the beaten track. Something really special. There are plenty of cruise liners calling into Wellington over the summer months. People with money who want a memorable day's experience. We'd give it to them for sure."

Paul pushed the glasses into a line, reached for the wine, and started to pour again. "It'll take a fair bit of that to cover the cost of the new machine."

"We'll be working it pretty hard," Erik said. "Some adventure survival treks for folk with tougher constitutions, too. That'll be Jawn's baby."

I was once again struck by the difference in their accents. Californian John, who pronounces his name 'Jarrn', and Erik who practically swallows the word. One of these days I'll ask Erik where he grew up.

"I'll fly them in," he continued, "And he'll lead them off into the wilderness and give them hell."

It was easy to imagine tall, tough John striding up impossible slopes and through impenetrable forest to make his team pitch tiny tents and cook what they'd caught or picked along the way. And wash in sparkling mountain streams.

I particularly enjoyed the pictures the last thought produced. Lovely fit people, wet bodies gleaming in the sun. Although what did I know? Somewhere recently I'd read wartime sailors in submarines didn't change their clothes or shower in months. Maybe John's lot would live on boring survival rations and emerge from the bush as smelly as the big leg of beef in Graham's car?

And just like that I'd wrecked the scene I'd conjured up!

Merry, you're a dork. Why do you let your brain run on so far?

"I'll drop a bunch of kayaks in to them if they want to run some rapids on the way out," Erik added.

Once again I was happily imagining shoulders in sunshine...

I watched as Paul handed the glasses of Merlot around. One corner of his mouth quirked as Heather had to let go of Erik's hand so she could reach across for hers. Big brother was definitely keeping his eye on little sister.

Erik raised his glass. "To the future," he said.

"And to making something for TV and YouTube that'll have people flocking to you," Heather replied, raising hers in return.

Ah – so this was presumably what they'd meant by 'front-woman' and 'scenery' and the other comments I'd managed to overhear.

"Yeah, she's no sooner landed in the country than I've stolen her," Erik said, clinking his glass against Heather's. "The gods of good fortune have dropped a beautiful actress into my lap, so I'd be mad not to make the most of her."

Paul sat back in his chair as though he had no intention of clinking anyone's glass. He frowned, looking far from pleased at the prospect of Heather falling into Erik's lap, literally or figuratively.

"So what do you think, Paul-James?" Heather asked. "If we shot a family segment would you be willing to play Dad?"

Paul gaped like a fish. "It's hardly appropriate for a

member of the clergy to turn up on TV advertising luxury helicopter tours!" He cleared his throat. "If it was fund-raising for Christmas hampers for disadvantaged people in the community that might be different."

Heather sighed, set her wine down, and left her chair to go and stand beside him. "You're such a straight-laced soul, aren't you, darling." She patted his hair, which incensed him more than soothed him. "We'd just need a nice tall dark man leading his little pretend family down to a pretty river. Shot from the back. Your face would never show."

Paul attempted to swat her hand away, but she smoothed it down the side of his head and bent and dropped a kiss on his brow. "Merry can be mother, and Erik says his helicopter mechanic has some photogenic children."

Goodness – I hadn't expected any sort of role! And doesn't the camera add a lot of weight? My tummy turned over at the thought, although if they were shooting from the back no-one would know it was me. Maybe I could wear a disguising floaty top, or more likely force my curves into the dreaded Spanx. "Lisa the vet has lovely children," I suggested. I knew how much Bailey, Mac and Pete would enjoy something like that; a free flight, and then to be slightly famous. "Two boys, one very pretty girl."

"That's them," Erik said. "Ten Ton's kids."

Now it was my turn to look astounded. "Ten Ton Smedley's your helicopter mechanic?" That didn't seem likely. Enormous Ten Ton ran the Drizzle Bay auto repair depot and was constantly covered in grease and short of cash. Vet

Lisa, his estranged wife, had the devil of a job getting any extra money out of him, and I happened to know she wanted some for a holiday sports camp for the children.

"Air Force background. Good guy. Trust him with my life."

I'm sure my eyebrows rose. "You have to if he's servicing your chopper."

Erik suddenly showed all his teeth in a blazing smile. "Quality friends or nothing, Merry."

Well, that didn't sound like an evil assassin; it smacked of something a vicar might say in one of his sermons.

"So you'll do it, won't you," Heather said firmly to Paul. "Only back view. We have plenty of other arrangements to make yet. I'm sure the kids will be keen."

He shook his head in a kind of wonderment. "Heather, you've been here *two days* and already you've got yourself involved with a murder and an acting job. He cast a glance sideways at Erik. "And possibly a man. How do you do it?"

Heather moved back to sit by Erik. "I'm not the least involved with the murder. And Erik and I have a purely business relationship," she declared.

I watched as he covered her hand with his again. Yeah, right. Purely business.

"You forget, darling," she insisted to Paul, "I spent the last ten years terrified Rob was going to die. I've been living at half-speed for ages. Worse for the last year after he was gone because I loved him dearly and miss him heaps."

Paul's stern expression softened. "You have some time to

make up for – I get it. Just... go carefully." He glared at Erik. "And you look after her."

Erik inclined his head. So maybe peace had broken out between the two protective men? I couldn't help wondering if anyone would worry that much about me. For sure my ex, Duncan Skeene, never had. You couldn't count Graham. Brothers have to.

"I don't suppose you're free for dinner are you, Erik?" I asked.

He narrowed his very dark eyes as he looked back at me "Could be, sure could be."

I sipped my wine. "I've made a big lasagne – just that and salad. It feels odd asking someone who owns a café to come to dinner. It won't be anything special."

"Might be more special than you can imagine," he said. One dark brow lifted. Surely he was referring to Heather's company and not my cooking?

(Although I did have Iona's special Christmas pudding cupcakes, some of which might have a surprise in the center. They'd add a bit of class.) I was glad I'd bought one for Graham now, even though it looked like Erik would get to eat it instead.

We sat on idly drinking and chatting as the sun slid lower in the summer sky. Erik was full of helicopter facts. Heather swung the conversation toward the TV commercial at every opportunity. Paul was far more occupied with arrangements for the Drizzle Bay annual Christmas community lunch to be held under the shop verandas.

I wandered through to the kitchen every now and again, breathing in the hot oregano-and-tomato scented air, checking the state of the lasagne, and pulling it out of the oven once it was golden and bubbling on top. I'd cheated with one of those bags of salad, but chopped a couple of tomatoes into it and plenty of strips of the crunchy capsicums I'd found at the Mini-mart and some basil from the big plant that always does well on the sunroom window sill. It looked like quite a good effort by the time I'd finished.

The Merlot might not have been super-compatible with the avocado and vinaigrette starters, but no-one complained. It certainly went superbly with the lasagne though. There were enthusiastic sniffs, and closed eyes, and blissful expressions on faces, so I concluded I'd done well enough. Or maybe it was because the rest of the wine had disappeared in a flash? "I can find another bottle of something," I offered.

Erik shook his head. "Not for me. Driving tonight, flying tomorrow."

"We're walking," Heather said, looking hopeful.

"Come and see what else is in the pantry," I said to Paul, and we went back to the kitchen together. Graham keeps the spirits in the cabinet in the big front room. I keep the wine in the kitchen – or sometimes in the fridge of course, if it's white.

And so the evening progressed – all of us, except Erik, with a little too much wine inside us. Iona's Christmas pudding cupcakes were greatly enjoyed – especially by Paul and Erik who each found a liqueur chocolate tucked away in the hollowed out centers of theirs.

"How come the men get the treats?" Heather asked, sending Erik a flirty look.

"Have a taste," said, leaning across and planting a chaste but lingering kiss on her lips, which definitely ended with a flick of his tongue.

"Mmm," she said.

Paul cleared his throat.

No-one had ever kissed me as coolly as Erik did Heather. With no worries about anyone else looking on. Or as sweetly and slowly and downright hungrily. A little green-eyed monster started doing a jig on my shoulder.

7

GRAHAM IN A GOOD MOOD

"COFFEE?" I croaked, just as the dogs erupted in a storm of barking outside. My ever-reliable intruder alarm! I pushed to my feet and then heard the back door opening. If that was Graham he was very early.

And indeed it was. He'd no doubt seen the dining room lights on, because he came straight through to us. Manny and Dan pranced and whined and told him how much they'd missed him while he'd been in Melbourne, and to my surprise he pulled out one of the other dining chairs and sat, gazing around genially and looking flushed and relaxed.

What?

Don't say 'what', dear, our mother chided me silently.

"You're early," I said, as he rubbed the spaniels' ears and thumped their backs.

"Tail wind. They made up time. And Vic Farrington

doesn't have much regard for the speed limit. We shot home at supersonic speed."

I recovered my hostess manners after a couple of seconds. "You know Paul, don't you, Graham? This is his sister, Heather, who arrived from England a couple of days ago for some sunshine. And Erik Jacobsen from the Burkeville Bar. Erik – my brother, Graham."

Hands were shaken.

"You're looking... cheerful?" I suggested. "Good conference?" Any other day my anti-social brother would have given curt nods all round and disappeared.

"Excellent," he said, and to my surprise he picked up the second wine bottle which still had a couple of inches left in it.

"I'll get you a glass," I said.

"I probably shouldn't. Had a bit on the plane."

I looked back over my shoulder at him and grinned. "I think you *should*. You're nice and relaxed on it."

He leaned forward and patted the spaniels again, talking nonsense to them and clicking his tongue, enjoying their adoring whimpers and licks.

"Legal conference, was it?" Paul asked.

Graham straightened. "Coastal properties. Climate change. Rising sea levels. Restitution and so on. Huge problems to follow, because both New Zealand and Australia have a lot of coastal settlements." He glanced out at the ocean. "I'm glad this place is elevated a few feet and we have the road between us and the water. Should get us through until the end of the century."

I probably rolled my eyes. "There you go," I said, handing his glass over. "Anyway, the car's good now." To be honest I was amazed he hadn't dashed straight into the garage to inspect it when he arrived.

"I'll have a look in a mo," he said, taking a swig of his wine.

I caught Paul's eye and shrugged. This wasn't like Graham at all. Had he met someone at the conference who'd taken his mind off things?

I decided to make the most of his unexpectedly good mood. "So how do you think anyone unlocked it? Bruce Carver thought it might have happened while it was parked behind your offices."

Graham swirled the wine around in his glass, brow furrowed. "It has to be because of Perce Percy," he eventually said.

There's that name again.

"Old client," he added. "Goes back to Dad's time."

I nodded. "Jim Drizzle mentioned him recently."

Graham gave Manny a pat on the shoulder. "I've been doing some work for old Perce. He came into the office again on Friday. He's selling up. Retiring from farming. No-one to leave the place to."

"Is that going to mean another Chinese-owned dairy farm?" Paul asked.

"Possibly, possibly," Graham agreed. "Well, it's finalized

now so I don't suppose it matters if I tell you. Yes, part of Devon Downs will be converted into a feedlot dairying operation."

"More cows, more methane, more pollution," Paul said gloomily, sounding like a complaining local. Most of the Drizzle Bay farms have been mixed beef-and-sheep just about forever. The citizens are leery of change. I could already imagine the gossip around the shops and at the Burkeville. No-one would be pleased once this news got out.

"Not all bad though," Graham added. "Perce wanted to set aside an area of the farm in perpetuity so I've guided him through the Queen Elizabeth Trust process and now he has a nice piece of land protected forever. There's a very pretty lake, and some wetlands. Interesting wildlife. Even a few Canada geese. Amazing cliffs and caves in some of the gullies."

"Sounds beautiful," Heather said, and I could see the cogs turning in her brain. *Unspoiled scenery for TV commercial. Lake, caves, birds, trees...*

"And of course not suitable for dairying anyway," Graham added. "Too steep in places, too much forest. It's an ecological corridor for some bird species, apparently, and all fenced off now."

"When do the new owners take over?" Erik asked.

"Couple of weeks. The QE2 covenant is already finalized."

Erik glanced at Heather. "You thinking what I'm thinking?"

She nodded, and turned her big blue eyes on Graham. "I'm investigating making a TV commercial which has a couple of scenes of a family enjoying a visit to the country. Paul will be the dad, Merry the wife."

Graham looked somewhat stunned and swigged more wine.

"We're searching for suitable settings," she continued, "and this place sounds ideal. I can promise you it won't be identified. No tourists overrunning it afterwards. One day's work and we'll be gone. Do you think we could check it out?"

"No reason I couldn't ask Perce," Graham agreed, blinking at her estrogen-powered assault.

"If it's as lovely as you say?" she practically purred.

I caught Erik's slight grin. Goodness, she was good. Graham was toast.

He straightened his shoulders and gave another slow blink. "Yes, I'll call Perce tomorrow. I want to check on him generally because he seemed a bit dithery. It's well time he gave up the farm and moved into the retirement facility where he's bought a studio apartment. He tells me they have a decent bowling green and a Men's Shed where the chaps can get away from the women."

"Peace at any price," Erik agreed.

"Dithery?" I asked.

Graham set his empty glass down. "Bit of a mix-up with the cars. He's bought the same model Mercedes as me, although I can't imagine why he needs a big car like that.

I smirked to myself. *There's only one of you, too, Graham.*

"And," he continued, "When he left, he inadvertently picked up my smart-key from the desk. Toddled back upstairs again, apologizing profusely when he found it wouldn't work on his car. But I've had time to think about this and I suspect he didn't re-lock mine."

"You didn't check?" I asked. Graham is so darned particular he comments immediately on any of my 'sloppy habits'. Nice to have the chance to poke back at him for once!

"No – er – well, you know how it is. The phone goes. The next client arrives. It leaves your brain..."

This was delicious. Between a few drinks and Heather's attention Graham was blushing like a schoolboy.

Paul leaned forward. "But why would anyone expect his car to be in your parking lot? Always supposing the beef was intended for him and not you?"

"It does seem more likely they wanted Perce's car," I said, pressing a finger down on a few stray crumbs of my Christmas pudding cupcake and transferring them to my tongue. "Maybe someone knew Beefy Haldane was working for Perce and wanted to send a warning to him. Perce's car is presumably locked in a garage out at the farm – and it would be too easy to spot someone tampering with it out there because I'll bet the old boy's nearby most of the time. Maybe they followed him into the village, hoping to somehow do it here?"

"Bit of a long shot," Graham muttered.

"But your parking lot's not overlooked because of that big sycamore tree." I said. "It was just your bad luck that the cars are the same model and yours was unlocked. There had to be two men because it was huge and heavy. Two men carrying two corners each of that big piece of plastic it was laid on. Heaving it in and making themselves scarce in a hurry."

"Still seems flaky to me," he said, bending down to fondle Dan's soft chestnut ears. "But yes, I'll concede it's a possibility."

He was saved from any further grilling by a text arriving. He dug his phone out of his pocket and his eyebrows rose. "DS Carver, wondering if I'm home from Melbourne yet."

"Invite him around," I unwisely offered. Really, if I drink more than two glasses of wine I lose half my common sense.

Dan gave a regretful sigh as his ears were deserted.

"My cue to be off," Erik said. "Tasty meal. Good company."

Heather rose too. "I'll see you to the door. Back soon."

Paul glared after them, probably picturing another kiss.

Graham rang instead of texting. He never totally deserts his lawyer mode of wanting to get things settled and correct. The DS was 'in the area' and very keen to 'drop by for a quick chat'.

I took the opportunity to stack the remaining plates in a neat pile and set them on the sideboard on the tray. Better not disturb the lovers...

And, astoundingly, only a minute or two later, the front doorbell rang and there he was. Had he been lurking around the corner?

The spaniels did their customary bark-off, so Graham

grabbed their collars and I answered the door, showing the DS into the dining room seeing that's where Graham was. I sat down again, ready to be part of the discussion. Why not? It was me who'd found the quarter cow. Or bull.

He looked from me to Graham to Paul and back again. No doubt noticed the stack of plates and wine glasses. "Am I interrupting?" he surprised me by asking as he sank rather wearily onto a chair.

I shook my head. "Have you eaten yet?" I knew there was still a chunk of lasagne in the baking dish.

"Expect I'll be home in about an hour. A coffee would go down well though?" Goodness, he was sounding almost human. And smelling a great deal less stinky now his cologne had faded by the end of the day.

I rose to go and make it. "Talk to the men. We have a theory."

"I never doubted you would have, Ms Summerfield," he said. Was he being snarky?

To my relief there was no sign of Erik and Heather anywhere near the kitchen. I scooped the remaining lasagne into a bowl, gave it a whizz in the microwave oven, and found a fork.

The DS swallowed and nodded, apparently lost for words when I presented his impromptu supper. Maybe no-one was ever kind to him?

"Coffee coming up in a minute," I said. "Anyone else?"

Paul and Graham both said yes, so I grabbed the tray of

plates and glasses and off I went again, hoping I wouldn't miss anything.

And I almost did.

"His *son*?" Graham was saying as I returned. "Didn't know he had one. Perce never mentioned him."

Whose son? And what's he done?

I set the tray of coffees down, waving at them to help themselves. Paul took pity on me and said, "Did you know Haldane had a son?"

I sat. "How would I know that? I've never met him. The first I knew he existed was that notice I found in the car."

DS Carver stopped eating for a moment. He looked really hungry, poor man. "The body on the tree has been formally identified as David Hardacre Haldane, nineteen-year-old son of – "

"Beefy!" I exclaimed. "Grandson of either Perce Percy or Maisie Hardacre, or possibly both."

DS Carver coughed – either on his lasagne or this information – and cleared his throat. "Who's Maisie Hardacre?"

"Mrs Perce Percy of Devon Downs, but I was told that in confidence. She's dead now, anyway."

DS Carver took another mouthful, chewed, and swallowed. "And who told you, Ms Summerfield?"

I tapped the side of my nose. It was something our dad used to do when he had a secret.

"It's the Police asking," Graham said in a warning tone.

"And they can look it up and check it in the 'Hatches, Matches and Dispatches' files," I snapped. "I'm sure it's a matter of public record, but I won't pass on something that I was asked not to."

Bruce Carver surprised me by grinning faintly and loading his fork again. "Fair enough," he said. He must have been hungry enough to abandon his usual sharpness.

"So where does that leave things?" Paul asked. "We all know Beefy was seriously into drugs. And now his son's been found dead. Erik saw a couple of big cannabis plots up on Mason's Ridge. Maybe the notice in the car was warning Beefy to keep away from there? Or to keep his son away? He did mention Mason's Ridge to me at the Totara Flats church, although he was so high and drunk it was anyone's guess what he was really talking about."

"Finding Mr Haldane is proving a problem," DC Carver said with evident annoyance. "Can you solve that one for us too, Ms Summerfield?" What a smarmy tone for someone who'd given him food! He was asking with no expectation of a useful answer.

I clamped my teeth on my bottom lip and then couldn't keep quiet. "He's in an old cottage on Devon Downs – probably on the QE2 covenant land."

"And you know that *how*?" Graham demanded.

I stirred some sugar into my coffee. "Jim Drizzle told me. I think he and Perce go back a long way. Perce told Jim he'd just given Beefy a job keeping an eye on the wetland area and trapping stoats and possums and so on – being a kind of unofficial warden in return for free accommodation. To keep him out of the way. Perce was hoping a calm atmosphere might help him recover from the war trauma and the drugs."

I glanced across at Paul. If anyone knew about wartime trauma it was him. His church had assigned Paul to drowsy Drizzle Bay in the hope the bucolic country atmosphere would help with the PTSD he'd sustained from serving as a chaplain in Afghanistan. Plainly they couldn't have forecast two local murders in more or less as many months.

"He's not going to recover from drugs with a son willing to supply him," Paul said.

I shook my head. "But apparently he hasn't got one any longer."

Bruce Carver laid down his fork and remembered his manners. "Thank you Ms Summerfield. For the food and the information." He reached for his coffee.

"We haven't solved it yet," I said. "We know who the body was on the X, but that's about all so far."

"We know how my car must have been unlocked," Graham said.

Bruce Carver shot him a gimlet-eyed glance. Plainly there'd be more questions about that tomorrow!

"Yes," I agreed, rushing on, "but we don't know who hid the beef there, or why they chose to do such a strange thing. Or why it didn't work as a warning."

Graham held up a finger. "I'm betting they wanted Perce to give up Beefy's whereabouts and threatened to steal one of his stud bulls, butcher it, and put the bleeding leg of beef in the trunk of his prize possession – his new Mercedes – if he didn't tell them."

"Unless it was a cow," I said. I'd been thinking of it as a cow all along.

Graham made an impatient noise and kept right on going. "And of course they got no reaction from Perce because they put the beef in the wrong car, so they went ahead and killed Beefy junior to stop their cannabis being stolen."

"And with you away at your conference it wasn't discovered for days."

"All-round fail," Paul said. "But you're right – there's no indication of who did it." He raised a brow at Bruce Carver. "This is all supposition, of course. Maybe it wasn't them growing the cannabis on Mason's Ridge? Maybe the Haldane son wasn't stealing it? Maybe the rustlers didn't kill him after all? Unless the Police are keeping that under wraps for their own good reasons?"

The DS took another sip of coffee. "Progress is being made, Vicar," he said with a bland expression. "Not enough to arrest anyone yet and this now seems to have turned from a rustling case to a murder with drugs on the side. Never say there's not enough to keep us busy."

He swallowed the last of his coffee and pushed back his chair. "I'll be in touch with you separately if that's okay. Or Detective Wick will. Get things properly documented."

We all made noises of agreement, and from somewhere outside I heard the powerful rumble of John's truck starting up. Or Erik's truck. Or perhaps they had one each? Who'd know with those two?

"The Burkeville truck?" the DS asked. "It was there when I arrived." Yes, he had sharp eyes for sure. Black truck, dark night.

We all listened to it doing what sounded like a U-turn and burbling off into the distance as Heather re-appeared from the kitchen, looking dreamy and lacking her lipstick. Of course the lack of lipstick might have been because she'd been eating and drinking. I was probably pretty unlipsticked myself by now. Perhaps they really had been talking about making the possible TV commercial? Or maybe fat pink piggies were flying up and down Drizzle Bay Road...

The DS gave her an assessing once-over as he turned for the door.

"Paul's sister, Heather," I said as I opened it for him. I waited until he was out in the warm, dark air before closing it and returning to the dining room.

"What did I miss?" Heather was asking.

"Nothing at all," Graham assured her.

She bent and patted Manny, who was keeping close to his master in case he went away again. Wow – nice view down the neck of her T-shirt – had she intended that? Yes, I reckon so!

And of course this made Graham putty in her small capable hands all over again.

"That would be wonderful if you could get permission from the old farmer tomorrow," she said, glancing up at him.

"As there are children involved we can't shoot until school breaks up." She turned to me and straightened. "When do the Christmas school holidays start here?"

"Different for older and younger students," I said, checking the time on my watch. "Want me to ask their mother? Do we know if Erik has already mentioned it to Ten Ton?"

Heather took her seat again. "I'm sure he has. He'll be flying the other helicopter."

Crikey – the things you don't necessarily know about your friends. I knew Ten Ton was ex Air Force, but had always presumed he was a mechanic. He's a gigantic man. Tall and broad, but no way fat. Even so, he must weigh twice as much as little Lisa.

"Yes, that'd be good," Heather agreed. "And maybe I could have a word about clothes."

I'd parked my cell phone on the sideboard so I reached across for it and scrolled to Lisa. She answered almost immediately.

"I didn't wake you up then?"

She laughed at that. "No chance. I can't get this lot into bed until after nine."

I heard bang-crash action movie noises in the background and assumed the kids were watching TV. "It's about this filming job. I have Paul's sister, Heather, here with me now and she'd like a word with you. About clothes and so on."

"Put her on. I'd like to know more myself. Ten Ton wasn't exactly forthcoming with details."

I stifled a laugh. "I don't know there's much set in concrete yet. Is everything good with you? I haven't seen you for a few days." As I listened, the background noise died away so I assumed Lisa had taken the phone somewhere quieter.

"Everything's fine," she sighed. "More or less. My campaign to get Ten back home with us isn't working yet. We need some time away from the kids, and I want them to go to a sports development camp down in Christchurch. Partly because it will be good for them. Partly because it will give us some privacy to try and sort things out. But the camp's going to cost a heap and he needs to make a contribution to it. I don't know why he always claims to have no spare money."

"There might be some payment for the TV commercial?" I suggested. "Anyway I'll hand over to Heather and the two of you can sort things."

She took my phone and moved through to the privacy of the kitchen, leaving Graham and Paul and I to eavesdrop as best we could. Not a hard task as it happened – her voice would have projected many rows back in a theatre without a microphone.

Graham turned his empty wine glass around and around. "To summarize," he said, "we have beef in my car for no reason at all, so we can discount that. It should have been in Perce's car. We might have Perce being threatened by whoever killed Haldane junior. Or we might not, of course.

But who else would it be? He's sold the farm, so there won't be any pressure coming to bear from other land owners."

"Until they hear about it," I muttered. "But if it's a done deal then they're too late."

"So we're back to these unknown rustlers," Paul said. "We know someone has been stealing animals from Jim Drizzle. Are they doing it to Perce Percy, too?"

Graham looked blank. "He didn't say so, although that might be the least of his worries now he's sold."

"And who does the pot plantation belong to?" I asked. "Was Beefy junior headed in that direction to make off with someone else's stash or was he just messing around on the beach?"

Paul pushed his hair back off his forehead. "He could get up to Mason's Ridge on a dirt bike. Maybe he's got his own, or maybe he borrowed Beefy's? The one I saw at my church?"

I nodded. "So if he was laid out dead on that tree on the beach, where's the bike? Still there somewhere, or did whoever killed him make off with it? Always supposing that's where he was killed."

"We're in Police territory now," Graham said. "But when we get interviewed tomorrow, we could ask."

"DS Carver won't like that," I said as Heather strolled back into the dining room and handed my phone to me. "Did you see any sign of a motorcycle by the body?"

She shook her head. "There was no time to see anything much. Once Erik knew what we were looking at, he zoomed off."

"But we could ask him what he saw when he went back?" I pushed the phone at her.

"Got him on mine," she said with a smile, sitting and scrolling to him. "Long time, no see," she greeted him. "Can you pull over for a quick chat?" She was silent for a few seconds. "Okay, well I've just had a word with the children's mother and we've sorted clothes. Casual stuff, plus swim-suits, so that's done. And we're still talking here, of course. Merry's asking if you saw any sign of a motorcycle when you went back. Dirt bike?" She looked across at me, listening as he answered. "He says no. I'll put you on speaker," she added to Erik.

"So maybe whoever killed him took it," I said.

Paul ran his fingers and thumb up and down each side of his chin. "Unless he was dropped off by someone, but that doesn't really make sense, does it? And it would take ages to walk that far down the beach. Unless you cut through some of Drizzle Farm's paddocks."

Graham turned his coffee cup slowly around on his saucer, gazing into its empty depths. "Could two men, one riding pillion, have followed him if they suspected him of stealing their pot? And after shooting him on the beach, put him on the tree as a warning to anyone else. One of them could have ridden his bike back. Dumped it somewhere."

"Not likely anyone would be passing," Paul said.

"That's really a nasty thought," I agreed. "But I can't come up with anything better."

"So we might have a couple of killers on the loose,"

Graham said morosely. "Killing animals, and now killing people as well. I don't like this at all."

"You don't know for sure they're killing the animals," Erik said. "They might be selling them off alive."

"They killed at least one," Graham said. "How would they transport them anywhere else? They'd need a truck for the job. There are all the usual stock carriers on the roads, of course, given the time of year. Have any of you noticed someone out of place?"

I remembered our drive back from Burkeville and having to adjust the air intake of the Focus as we got too close to that old green truck. It might have been nothing but it did seem worth a mention. I looked across at Heather and Paul. "Do you remember that truck we were following this morning? Not sign-written as I recall, and it was pretty stinky."

"Dark green," Paul said. "Definitely for transporting stock, but I don't recall any name on it. Might be nothing. Do any of the farmers have their own trucks?"

This time it was Graham's turn to stroke his chin. "It would be unusual. Transporting cattle and sheep is specialized work. I can see it's a possibility if farmers want to ferry stock from one property they own to another on a regular basis – to make the most of available feed and so on – but I'd lay odds they'd be using professionals to take them to the meat processing plants."

We all nodded agreement.

"They'll have the usual farm runabouts and all-terrain vehicles of course," he added, "but not often anything larger.

Sometimes maybe a trailer with a cage if it's only a couple of beasts."

Erik's deep voice rumbled out of the phone again. "Too public to tow that behind a pick-up. You'd see what they were carrying. Heather – do you want to ride shotgun with me tomorrow morning if we get permission to do some aerial surveillance from that old farmer? Two pairs of eyes are better than one."

Heather gave a grudging laugh. "Unfortunate description, 'riding shotgun'."

"Yeah – wasn't a shotgun that killed that kid, though. One rifle shot to the chest."

"Don't," she said softly.

8

CROSS COUNTRY

Erik, being Erik, decided he could fly over anything he wanted to without waiting for permission.

"So are you on for reasonably early in the morning?" we heard him drawl. "Maybe about 8.30? I have things to do later."

"And I suppose you'll both have to talk to Carver or Wick," Paul said.

Heather puffed out an impatient breath. "They can wait. I really can't tell them anything more than Erik already did."

"You got transport or you want me to collect you?" he asked.

She looked across at Paul. "Is your car fixed yet?"

"With any luck I'm collecting it from Ten Ton by midday – he was waiting for a replacement radiator."

"I can take you," I said. I remembered Erik and John and Heather had all shared the first flight. Why not Erik and

Heather and me this time around? "So we come to Kirk-patrick's barn around 8.30?"

"Okey-dokey," Erik said, although no actual invitation to fly was issued. Surely he wouldn't be so cruel as to leave me standing by the barn while he flew off with Heather?

"You know where you're going?" Graham asked. That was aimed at Erik, not me.

"Yup – pulled it up on the sat-map."

"Devon Downs," Graham said, wanting to make sure.

"Yup – can see the lake. Might have to land outside the fenced area if we do this for real. There's a lot of native forest."

"Bush," Graham said.

"Bigger than bushes! But yes, I know that's what you Kiwis call it."

"No idea why," I said. "But it's the areas of original native vegetation. For instance, you wouldn't call that pine planta-tion 'bush'."

"And over in Aussie," Graham added, "They call every-thing outside the cities 'bush', and it's mostly open space with damn-all bushes."

"Strange world, Down Under," Erik agreed with a smile in his voice. "Anyway, we'll have a look in the morning, and if it's not suitable then no point even asking the owner."

"I'll be phoning him anyway," Graham said. "See how he's coping."

"Leave it until maybe ten," Erik said. "I'll get back to you."

Then he changed to a much softer tone. "You want to take me off speaker now, honey?"

Heather reached out for the phone. "Done," she murmured. "So I'll see you in the morning."

I watched as she closed her eyes and listened to whatever private things he wanted to say. Then she gave a quiet laugh, said 'you too,' and disconnected.

———

I'D PROMISED myself Thursday was the day I'd spend time on Elaine O'Blythe's next animal opus – sorting out the spelling and the alarming liberties she sometimes took with her grammar. She's a charming storyteller though, and this time it was another tale about Kerry the kereru. But was Kerry the big pigeon going to take precedence over a possible helicopter flight? Not on your nelly!

I grabbed a slice of toast and marmalade, gave my desk a guilty glance, called goodbye to Graham through the bathroom door, and was on the road in my Ford Focus by eight o'clock. Five minutes later I was knocking on Paul's glossy red front door. Heather and I made it to Kirkpatrick's barn with time to spare but Erik had beaten us there. He was using his very strong body to pull a small wheeled platform out of the barn, and on top of it sat the helicopter. It didn't seem right one man could move something so heavy, but he assured us there were really good bearings in the trolley wheels so he didn't need help.

I locked the car, hoping if I looked as though I expected to join them I wouldn't be turned down. And sure enough...

Erik pulled the barn's big door closed. "Heather in the middle," he said. "You here, Merry." He slapped the seat next to Heather. Once I was in and he'd secured the door he strode around to the pilot's side, made sure we were buckled in to his satisfaction, and handed us each a rather clunky set of headphones with a little microphone attached. "It'll be noisy," he said. "Make sure they're tight." He insisted on checking, and showed me how to push mine another notch tighter, leaning all over Heather to reach me. She kissed his neck.

"No distracting the pilot," he said, pulling back and patting her leg. He pushed her microphone back in front of her mouth and was very businesslike after that. His voice crackled in my ears once the rotors were whomping around and he had things running as he wanted. "Flight plan filed. Weather fine with no surprises expected. Good to go." And we went. Straight up – slowly to start with, and then as we climbed, more and more of Kirkpatrick's farm lay spread below us. You could sense the enormous power in the machine from the way it vibrated, wanting to be up in the sky where it belonged.

Cattle and sheep galloped away from the noise, stopping comically in lines as they reached the fences. Off to the left the ocean glittered under the brilliant sun, and the main highway and the Burkeville with its parking lot in front were easy to find. No customers' cars at this early hour, but a couple of staff vehicles showed at the back.

I peered down, watching the fields and fences and trees pass by below us and getting a look at farmhouses normally hidden from view. I'm sure I spotted Old Bay Road where the crafting conference at Horse Heaven had been. They were due to have their pre-Christmas sale this weekend. I must ask Heather if she'd like to come with me. It'd be a good place to find gifts to take home to England. "See that place?" I said, nudging her. "With the big oval track? Remind me to tell you something later."

The countryside crawled by. Drizzle Bay village looked like a model from the air; the main street with all the shops and Paul's church, and even the Summerfield residence in the row of houses over the road from the ocean. The tiny shapes of Manny and Dan raced around the back lawn, probably barking at us. This was magic!

I was amazed how many people had swimming pools even though they lived at the beach. Turquoise circles and rectangles sparkled in the sun behind quite a number of the houses.

We shuddered on – pretty much along Drizzle Bay Road. I hadn't really expected so much noise and vibration, but I guess it takes a lot of power to pull a helicopter and three people into the air and keep them safely up there.

We passed Lisa's vet clinic and I was surprised to spot washing flapping on a line in the yard behind it. From the air the place was quite big. I'd never been to her home. It looked as though she and the children lived on the premises because the washing definitely included clothes, large and small, and at least one pair of sheets billowing in the breeze.

"That's where Lisa and your TV kids live," I said, pointing. I felt bad I hadn't known that. I sometimes saw Lisa at Lurline's Animal Rescue place when I walked dogs for her, and occasionally around the village and at the Burkeville Bar and Café, or at Iona's bakery. I counted her as a friend, and I hadn't known where she lived? Shame on me. She'd never invited me home, although when I thought about it I'd never invited *her* home, either.

The agricultural tanks place looked amazing from the air. The yard behind the main building was studded with circles and squares in assorted sizes and colors – plainly they stocked tanks for many purposes.

Erik's voice crackled in my ears again. "I'm heading along to where we spotted the body yesterday in case I can see the bike you were wondering about last night. You might want to close your eyes when we get nearer until I give you the all clear."

No – it was far too thrilling to close my eyes, and surely they would have removed poor Beefy junior by now? An unbroken area of sand and waves stretched below us.

We slowed, and Erik pointed downward. A little way ahead lay the weathered white tree trunk. It was easy to imagine it as a cross with its two big side-branches. "They've taken him away," Erik said.

"Thank heavens for that," Heather replied. "It was an awful thing to do to someone."

"So – you see any sign of a motorcycle from up here?" he asked.

Sunshine wasn't gleaming off handlebars or chrome trim anywhere, and even if the bike was filthy we might have expected a stray flash or sparkle to give it away if anyone had tried to hide it. The gusty wind can really move sand around, and the helicopter's rotors even more so.

"The murderer must have ridden off on it," Heather said.

"If there ever was a bike." Erik turned the machine in a slow circle. "Looks like wheel ruts in the sand down there."

I glanced across at him. "But if the Police have done all they need to do – retrieving the body and searching the area closely for any possible clues – they would have had vehicles here. Those could be anyone's ruts. Maybe they found the bike?" That was a question for DS Carver later today. "And back there's the old cottage where I looked after the dogs when Isobel was killed," I said, pointing sideways.

Erik changed direction so we flew right over it. "Yeah, the place Jawn's keen on buying for the surfing."

"Not a chance right now with Margaret Alsop living there. The lady with the poodle who called in at the Burkeville," I reminded Heather. "It's about all she has left, poor thing."

"Yup – Tom Alsop was neck-deep in deception," Erik agreed. "She has a visitor." A white pick-up truck crouched beside the garage, hidden from the road, although Drizzle Farm and the old cottage were the very last places along here and traffic was sparse at best.

"Maybe it's a lawn-mowing contractor?" I suggested. "There's a big lawn – well, a big stretch of grass – too much for one elderly woman to keep under control. I know one of the boys from Drizzle Farm used to mow it for forty bucks because he did it while I was there."

Erik made a non-committal noise. "No-one seems to be mowing anything yet."

"And that's Drizzle Farm," I added for Heather's benefit. "Owned by Lord James Drizzle and Lady Zinnia. Bet you didn't expect to find a genuine English Lord all the way down here at the end of the world?"

Heather sent me a cheeky grin. "Paul's already told me about how Lord Jim inherited the title because he was the last survivor in the family. I gather he's as Kiwi as they come?"

I nodded. "Old friend of my father," I said, inspecting the assorted farm buildings – the main farmhouse, the barns and implement sheds, the olive green bus half hidden under a tree, and several smaller houses where staff lived. And a swimming pool, because a ready source of water is important for fire-fighting in rural areas. Then the glinting river came into view. Somewhere along its banks Alex had found Isobel Crombie's wrecked computer and liberated the hard-drive for DS Carver. I couldn't help wondering if he'd have handed it in if he'd known it would help send his birth father to prison.

We watched the long breakers rolling in and sliding up

the wide sandy beach. Then Erik turned further inland and headed toward the hills.

Devon Downs sounds as though it's set on rolling English countryside, but that's misleading. Yes, there was a lot of flat ground where a very grand house had been built in the fifties or sixties. Mid-century modern I suppose you'd call it.

"Not many brick houses in New Zealand," Heather said, looking down on the sprawling white weatherboard building.

I couldn't help laughing. "We get a few earthquakes. The timber houses are flexible. Bricks and masonry don't always survive the big ones."

"Awful thought," she said. "Look at all those French doors out to the decks and patios. What a party pad."

There seemed to be no-one around so Erik flew right overhead which gave us an excellent view down to a big central atrium with a glittering swimming pool and timber loungers arranged on the surrounding paved area.

"There's the party pad in the middle," I said. "A really sheltered sun-trap, and what a place to invite friends to. So private they wouldn't even need clothes!"

Heather got the giggles at that, and even Erik cracked a laugh. "Remind me not to come to parties with you," he said. "But yep – quite a place. It'd be hard to leave it."

There was still no sign of anyone, either close to the house or to any of the farm buildings. Maybe Perce was still in bed? "I think the old guy was lonely," I said. "Widowed a while ago. And no children, except possibly Beefy, and no proof of that. I'm sure if he thought he had a son to leave the farm to, he would have."

In the fields surrounding the house dozens of cattle grazed. Then a four-wheeler farm bike zoomed out from a shed partly hidden under trees. Black and brown dogs bounded around it and I saw the bike slow so the rider could move an electric fence wire. The stock immediately raced through to the area of new feed, a closely packed flow of lumbering beasts. Plainly they had no faith their field-mates wouldn't instantly eat every blade of green before they could get to it.

Further back a range of hills rose up steeply, studded with sheep. The sheep panicked as we drew closer, running from the helicopter's noise and then stopping just as suddenly as we left them behind.

"Silly things," Heather said.

Erik climbed, and soon we were past the top of the hills and into a different world. "I'm guessing this is the area that can't be farmed," he suggested, slowing the machine so we could see everything better. "The protected part. Looks like original forest to me."

The valley was beautiful – with untold shades of green woven together into a continuous patchwork of trees. Hundreds of paler green circles showed where tall tree-ferns had made their homes. Stands of dense, dark manuka spread down to a sparkling lake bordered by clumps of strap-leaved flax, tussock, and rushes. Tall stalks of toi toi waved their fluffy pennants of seed, and a small stream glinted like diamonds as it flowed out at one end.

"Let's see where that goes," Erik said. "Can either of you spot any signs of civilization?"

Heather and I both peered down. Nothing but virgin native bush. Although... "Is that smoke?" I asked. "Just past that very tall tree poking up over there?"

"Could be," Heather said. "Or just a drift of morning mist?"

Erik kept flying straight ahead. "Don't want to spook anyone by hanging around. I'll make it look like we're flying past, and come back the same way in a few minutes. I think you're right about the smoke. Something small and controlled. Not trees on fire. Might be where Haldane's hanging out."

"Jim said Perce had offered him an old cottage," I said. "Maybe they didn't like it and set up camp there instead? I'm presuming he still has Roddy in tow, although Perce might not know that."

"Where did the son live?" Heather asked.

I shook my head. "We don't know. We're only presuming they were even in touch with each other."

"Not any longer," Erik muttered. He flew on, high over the stream, and Heather gasped as it poured over a ledge of rock in a lacy white waterfall. "Perfect place for your commercial," she said. "And would there be room to land over that side?"

The ground was flatter here. Flat enough to drive on, to

judge by the rough wheel-ruts that led in from a fence on the far side. "And we've found it," Erik said, pointing to the small high-sided stock truck parked mostly under a big evergreen tree covered with scarlet flowers.

"Pohutukawa," Heather said slowly, getting the pronunciation pretty close. "Your New Zealand Christmas tree."

Erik dipped the nose of the machine so we could see the ground better. Heather and I both squealed and clutched our harnesses, and he chuckled. "They must have cut the fence – unless there's a gate there. And if this is still the land that's protected then there shouldn't be anyone on it, should there?"

"I'll ask Graham," I said. "But yes, I think they're trespassing. He did say the QE2 covenant was all finalized."

Erik climbed higher. "I'll turn back in a couple of minutes," he said as the land rose at the end of the valley. "There's a building there," he added, pointing at a shape overgrown with creepers and branches.

"Good eyes!" Heather exclaimed. "That's really hard to see."

"So we have two possible sites of habitation," he said. "I'm betting Haldane was the smoke, and your other people are hanging out down there, closer to their truck."

"Not *my* people," I said. "And if Beefy was told he could have the cottage, maybe they've fought over it? This gives us something for Graham to ask old Perce, and something for me to tell DS Carver. Unless you want to?"

Erik shook his head and grunted, not looking me in the eye. Huh? What was he hiding?

"Okay, I'll do it," I said as we flew on over more paddocks of lolloping pale sheep.

A few minutes later he turned in a wide circle and retraced the route. "Can either of you take a few photos? Handy for the Police, but also a good reference for the filming."

Heather and I both produced our phones. "You want me to use yours?" she asked him. "I'll bet it's better than mine."

I heard him chuckle as he handed it over. We spent the next little while framing up views and clicking away. All too soon Erik was losing height over Kirkpatrick's farm again, lowering us slowly down onto the trolley so he could pull the machine back into the barn.

"Coming back for a coffee?" he asked as he re-locked the barn door and Heather and I stood enjoying the sun and checking the photos we'd taken. There was a big buddleia bush there, branches dripping with fragrant purple flower fronds. It was covered in bees and butterflies, and I inhaled the sugar-sweet scent as I watched a couple of big orange and black Monarchs fluttering around the blooms. It's not known as 'the butterfly bush' for nothing.

Erik's invitation reminded me I'd told Iona I'd bring Heather in to see about pre-Christmas work although I hadn't made an actual time to do it.

"Tea for me," Heather said before I could mention Iona. Ah

well, it was barely nine-thirty yet. We could easily have a cup with Erik now and one with Iona a little later. First of all I needed to phone Graham and let him know about the intruders in the protected part of Devon Downs. I guessed he'd tell Perce, or maybe Perce would ask if he'd phone the Police for him.

Heather had made her way toward Erik's pick-up so I said, "Go with him and I'll catch up with you. I'll let Graham know about the stock truck being where it shouldn't be."

I'd called goodbye to him through the bathroom door, but apart from that I hadn't seen or heard him this morning. He'd been running later than usual; could he possibly have a hangover? I decided I'd try his cell phone and avoid spending time chatting with his secretary, Jenny Henderson. She's very nice, but she's worked for him so long she kind of counts herself as one of the family and feels inclined to ask personal questions I don't always want to answer.

Two rings. "Merry!" Graham barked. "Where are you?"

"I said goodbye. You were in the bathroom."

"Might not have heard you over the electric toothbrush."

"Not my problem! You knew where I was going. We talked about it last night. For a look at Devon Downs in Erik's helicopter."

"Ah. Yes. And you've been?" He was definitely sounding tetchy.

"Yes." I opened the driver's side door of the Focus and sat down. "Lovely morning for it, but I need to ask something. It's the valley with the lake that's now protected and out of bounds, isn't it? So there shouldn't be anyone there?"

Graham cleared his throat. "Apart from Beefy Haldane."

"Yes, we saw a bit of smoke that might be him. But further along we also saw an old stock truck mostly hidden under a tree. I'm sure it's the one we saw yesterday and talked about at dinner. Dark green. There were wheel-tracks leading across to a rough farm road at one end. We weren't sure if there was a gate or if they'd cut the fence. I can send you a photo."

"Yes please," Graham said. "Definitely shouldn't be there. Could you see people?"

I pulled the sun visor down because it was getting really bright. "No, but Erik spotted a building quite close to the truck. Covered over with trees and so on. Good hiding place, so probably. Unless that's where Beefy is."

"DS Carver needs to know about this," Graham said. "And Perce."

I wanted my coffee at the Burkeville. And I wanted to watch Erik and Heather romancing each other for a while longer because they were just delicious together. "I'll send you some photos," I said firmly. "You're the one with the QE2 covenant info, so you ring them both and tell him. Bye." And I disconnected. Too bad if that didn't suit him. I transferred the best of the photos to his phone and started the engine.

Erik had driven slowly out onto the road, and when he saw my car moving he picked up speed. I rattled out over the cattle-stop bars and followed his smart black truck to the Burkeville. It took only three or four minutes. There were already several other vehicles in the roadside parking lot so that made a long day for them. No wonder they had a variety of staff to cover all the hours.

We walked in together, and I froze. Prickles of heat and cold fizzed along my spine. Duncan Skeene! Side-on enough that he didn't see me, but I could certainly see him. And also see the disconcertingly young woman gazing across the table at him.

9

OLD SCORES

"Somewhere further back," I hissed at Erik.

"Why?" Heather asked.

"My ex-husband. Over by the window." I attempted to indicate him with my chin. Other customers were outside enjoying the sunshine, but not my philandering former spouse.

"Really?" Heather asked, giving him a thorough inspection.

Erik shepherded us sideways. "Who's the spring chicken?"

I rolled my eyes at him. "No-one I know – or want to know. He's a horrible womanizer. That's why I finally gave him the push."

"She's half his age," Heather whispered.

"Possibly," I muttered.

Erik maneuvered us to a table where we were out of

Duncan's line of sight but could still see his back. And her rather flat front. "Tea for you, honey?" Erik asked. "And coffee for you?" He bent closer and really surprised me by murmuring, "Maybe I can rustle up a pretty blond Californian who looks like he's pleased to see you?" His eyebrows rose over his dark eyes. Eyes full of wicked glee.

I certainly hadn't expected that. I'd only ever seen Erik as serious, secretive, totally concentrating on whatever he was doing. Perhaps he was softening a little with Heather's attention?

I blew out an annoyed breath, loving the idea but not expecting it to happen. "Duncan's not worth the effort."

"Oh, I don't know..." Erik continued. "Looks like he deserves it and you'd enjoy it."

I shrugged, and shook my head. "Haven't seen him in a couple of years, but he hasn't changed his spots."

Erik left us and I reached for one of the little packets of sugar stacked in a bowl in the center of the table. I turned it around and around, bouncing it on its corners, distracted and far more annoyed than I wanted to be. My tummy felt sour and then squelchy. My fingers longed to drop the packet and close around my ex-husband's neck instead. And squeeze. It was hard to keep my distaste for him off my face, but the last thing I wanted was for him to spot me looking discontented without him.

He'd be forty-seven now. His hair was thinning on top, and the edges appeared a suspiciously brighter shade of brown than I remembered. He still looked in reasonable shape – as much as I could judge from the back, and with him sitting down. He said something to the girl, and she laid a hand on his arm and gave an over-loud laugh I wouldn't want to hear too much of. Maybe he didn't mind it?

"How long were you married?" Heather whispered, glancing across at them.

"Too long. Years too long." I pulled a face. "Total waste of my thirties. I should have ended things years earlier." Then I leaned closer to her. "But I guess I loved him once, and you don't like admitting you've made a huge mistake."

Heather wrinkled her nose. "I was lucky," she said. "Rob and I were a total love-match for as long as we lasted. We knew his health was precarious for years, and we lived every day as fully as we could."

I nodded slowly as I thought about that. "Better those really good years than a whole lot of mediocre ones."

"Yes, that's how I decided to think about it," she said. "I didn't have him forever, but I had him fully and lovingly. I'm so grateful for that."

Was I jealous? Much? Moving on... "And who knows what the future will bring?" But it obviously wasn't the time to tease her about Erik so I changed the subject. "I have something to ask you. Feel free to say no."

Heather grinned and raised her eyebrows. "Okay, I'll bite."

"No, it's nothing much. But Paul said you were a keen baker – almost entered The Great British Bake-Off?"

She dropped her gaze from mine. "Yes, but Rob dying knocked the stuffing out of me at just the wrong time."

I bit my lip. This was hard. She was so obviously still hurting. "Understandable," I murmured. "We have a really good bakery here – you had the Christmas pudding cupcakes from there last night."

Heather nodded. "They were delicious."

"Iona is a good friend, and run off her feet pre-Christmas. I cheekily mentioned you, and wondered if you might like to meet her and maybe do a bit of work there. But of course that was before the filming thing happened."

"Working in a bakery?" Her big blue eyes positively glowed.

"It's only a little place. Don't go expecting anything too much. But I didn't know if Paul was going to tie up all your time or if you'd maybe be at a loose end sometimes...?"

"I'd love to," she exclaimed. "To be honest I was wondering what I'd do while he's busy this close to Christmas. I was thrilled when the filming thing came up, but that won't be happening right away."

"With such a nice man attached," I couldn't help teasing.

"He is, isn't he," she said with a grin. "Probably come to nothing, but I'll take it while it lasts."

"You never know," I said. It's true. You never do. "Anyway," I added, "Sometime later this morning we could go and meet Iona. Maybe buy something for lunch. We can find out what she might need help with, and if you'd be interested in doing it."

"Or capable of it," Heather inserted.

"I don't think there'll be any trouble with that," I murmured, still keeping half an eye on Duncan's back and picturing myself through his eyes. I'd put some decent jeans on, and a T-shirt that had a skyscraper design because it seemed to go with an American helicopter pilot. My hair was up in a messy bun and I'd given it a quick tidy after the headset came off. I wasn't looking my worst, but I wasn't looking my total best, either. Then again, the girl he was with had youth on her side but terrible glittery earrings that seemed weird for a beach café, and ultra-whitened teeth that dazzled as much as the earrings.

"I mustn't take up all your time," Heather said. "I know you're busy, too."

I put the packet of sugar down and took a deep breath. "Yes, but I work my own hours, and people are mostly pretty good. If I don't like their attitude or their writing then I don't do repeat jobs for them. My dyslexic lady, Elaine, is total fun. She always scans her paintings and sends them too, so I know what she's trying to describe. Editing something like a translated engineering catalogue can be a hard slog. Lord Drizzle is writing his memoirs and that's going to be an adventure sometime next year."

Her eyebrows went up. "What – about being a farmer?"

"And a motorcycle racer in his youth. He said he wanted to do it for his family, but he's always been a bit of a storyteller. And then of course finding out he was a Lord..."

She nodded, looking thoughtful. "Could be quite interesting, then. But you mostly do books?"

I was about to confirm that when there was an exuberant yell of, "Merry! Babe! You're back from The Big Apple!"

John came striding toward the table with my coffee, looking entirely too delighted to see me. A great, tall, tawny beast of a man, snake-hipped, with a torrent of long sun-streaked hair, and so much more athletic than Duncan could ever be. John's certainly less than Ten Ton's six foot seven, but appreciably more than Graham's five-eleven. As his hair was down I assumed he'd intended going surfing. Maybe Erik had insisted he dragged those tight black jeans on over his board-shorts to do this bit of play-acting?

At the sound of my name Duncan turned in his chair. I avoided his inspection and gazed up at John, eyes wide open and boobs up-thrust, thinking I may as well play to my strengths. He set down the coffee and cupped my face in both big hands. I half expected he was going to plant a smacker of a kiss on my surprised lips. I wouldn't have minded. In fact I would have quite liked it.

Up close he smelled amazing – of hardly anything at all, but I wanted to get closer and maybe work out what it was. And his lips had those *edges* that some mouths do – kind of well-defined and totally kissable.

But no... Instead he held my face as though I was treasure, brushing his thumbs over my cheekbones. He also sent me a sexy wink which Duncan wouldn't have seen.

He gazed down at my boobs and then up into my eyes

again as I sat there hypnotized and sniffing him. "Loooooove your skyscrapers," he said. *That* was when the kiss happened. Not a smacker. A kiss longer and more lingering than Erik had given Heather so she could sample his liqueur chocolate the evening before. Possibly the best kiss I'd ever had. Gentle but firm. Definitely exploratory, which no-one else would have seen, but I could feel for sure. More of a kiss than was called for in the situation, but was I going to push him away?

For some reason, no. In fact I grabbed his long hair to stop him escaping. Buried my fingers in it and dragged my lips gently over his one more time, hoping he'd do the same in return so the kiss lasted even longer. And he did.

But dammit, I hadn't meant to do that. I hadn't meant to nip his bottom lip either. Or slide my fingers around to the back of his head, enjoying the soft warmth of his hair against the skin of my arms.

We finally pulled apart. I was panting slightly. John is so darn fit I don't think anything would make him pant.

Job well done, Mr California! Just like that I was a world traveler and the object of enthusiastic admiration from a handsome hunk.

"John," I gasped with a lot less panache than I'd hoped for. "Great to see you again too."

From the corner of my eye I registered Duncan scowling and turning back to his date and Erik approaching with Heather's tea.

"For our English Rose," Erik said, blocking out my view

of Duncan and allowing me to draw a couple of fast, desperate breaths.

"Thank you for the coffee – and everything," I said after John had finally stood to his six feet whatever.

"Sounds like you found some interesting 'friends'?" He said that with a lift of one eyebrow so I understood he meant the stock-truck intruders. Duncan would have surmised something entirely else. Heaven knows what. Did I even care?

"It's amazing what you can see from a helicopter," I agreed.

I sensed Duncan looking around at us again, but I kept my eyes up on John's slightly flushed face.

"Nice to have you home safe," he said. "Talk later." And he strode back to the kitchen area and disappeared, leaving me bathed in the glow of his overwhelming masculinity. I fear I was grinning like an idiot and clutching at my chest to try and calm the hectic beating of my adolescent heart.

Erik folded onto the chair beside Heather. I could see what Paul meant about him being light on his feet despite being thick with muscle. He moved like a cat – unnervingly flexible for someone so strong.

My pair of Black Ops men. Could they really be? Did I care? I'd planned to pull old Isobel Crombie's file down from Dropbox and have a really good read again this evening. Unless, of course, they were Tom Alsop's files.

Actually, why would either of them have a file about Black Ops assassins? I couldn't see Isobel searching for anything like that. How to grow dahlias or the best food for parsnips, maybe. And car-dealer Tom Alsop seemed only a little more likely. Maybe the awful Nam Cheng had more access to their shared computer than I knew about? Oh well, he was probably banged up in a horrible prison in his homeland after being deported, so for sure he wouldn't be logging in any more.

I'd already tried quizzing DS Bruce Carver about John and Erik and got a series of mumbles and throat-clearings and nothing sensible at all. Enough to make me suspicious they were in some sort of cahoots. Although what?

I turned my attention to Erik and Heather as she whispered something to him and he touched her hair, running a finger slowly along the pale strands. "Yeah, we'll keep it there, too," he said. "That place has a lot more security than anyone will expect."

I presumed he was talking about the barn on Kirkpatrick's farm. "For the new one?" I asked. "When do you get it?"

He wound the strand of her hair around and around his finger and gazed back at Heather as though I was invisible. "That's what I'm busy with any moment now and why we had to go early today." He released her hair and I heard him sigh. "So I'll see you both in a couple of days, and then we'll get to work."

"Miss you," she said, narrowing her eyes at him. "Stay out of trouble."

He gave her a much quicker kiss than John had just given

me. "Count on it." He rose and strode away, and I watched her watching him until he was out of sight. Then I picked up the well-handled little packet of sugar, tore it open with more force than necessary so the grains showered everywhere, and tipped the remainder into my coffee.

Heather stayed silent as she turned her teapot to and fro. "You and John?" she finally asked.

"It was a fake."

She pursed her lips. "A very high quality fake?"

I screwed up the empty sugar packet. Tightly. And watched the questions flicker in her eyes.

She poured out a cup of tea and set the teapot down again. "Not you and Paul, then?"

Hmmm. Tricky. "Paul's made it plain he's not ready for a relationship with anyone yet." I hoped that would deflect her.

She was no fool. "That wretched war," she said. Softly. Bitterly. "Politicians don't see the downhill tragedies. Paul went there to help and he was just about killed. Not with guns, but with unrelenting mental stress." She covered her mouth with a hand. Closed her eyes for a few seconds and then looked at me again. "I'm glad he has people like you in his life."

I took a deep breath and let it out. "Two murders here in the last couple of months. Possibly not the ideal environment after what he's gone through. Not that anyone was expecting them, of course. We have the occasional hunting accident and some awful road smashes but not much else." I held my tongue for a few seconds and then couldn't help myself. "Did he tell you his prints were on the murder weapon of the first one?"

Her eyes shot wide open. "No! Surely he wasn't under suspicion for it?"

She looked so appalled I wished I hadn't mentioned it. "Not at all. In fact he was the missing link to solving it, in a strange way. Let him tell you sometime."

She relaxed again and I felt terrible for worrying her. Taking one of the paper napkins from the holder in the center of the table I brushed the sugar grains into a small heap. "What a mess," I said, trying to dab it up, and then wondering where to put it. In the end I laid it flat, added the little sugar packet and twisted them up together. "Have you had breakfast?"

Heather shook her head. "I'm still all at sea, time-wise. I really didn't expect that long flight would knock the stuffing out of me quite the way it did."

"Do you want something from here? I only had a tiny piece of toast – partly because of the early start, and partly because I was excited about flying and thought a full stomach might not be a good idea. I bet Erik and John both ate hours ago." I glanced at my watch. "Or we could go and have something at Iona's so you can meet her?"

Her big blue eyes really lit up at that thought. "Yes please. You probably think baking is a strange ambition after acting but it's something I've always adored."

I took a sip of my coffee. "Each to their own. I've always

loved dogs. I dog-walk sometimes for the animal shelter. And I have a house-and-pet sitting service for people if they're on holiday or maybe in hospital. It gets me away from Gloomy Graham."

Heather clapped a hand over her mouth to stifle a laugh. "He's not!"

"Granted he wasn't last night. He'd either got into the drinks on the plane or he met someone in Australia and did a bit of flirting. He's generally much more morose. I hope this murder doesn't throw him back into serious mode again."

She tilted her head and rested her elbow on the table and her chin in her palm. "Anyone would be serious, knowing there was a murderer on the loose. Especially if there was a great chunk of cow left in your car. I wonder where the rest is?"

I rolled my bottom lip in over my teeth and took a deep breath. "This is nastier than Isobel's murder. That poor boy was so young. And leaving him laid out like that is peculiar and spooky."

We shrugged in unison, tipped our drinks up for a last sip, and put them down at the same instant.

"Twins," Heather said, glancing from cup to mug. "Anyway, you said to remind you to tell me something – about the place that looked like it had a dressage ring?"

I glanced across to where Duncan Skeene and his youthful companion were just scraping back their chairs and deserting their table. Once they'd moved away a few steps, I said, "Horse Heaven. There's a handcrafts sale there this weekend. I wondered if you might like to go and have a look. For gifts to take home, maybe?"

Heather wrinkled her nose. "It's too early to be thinking about that, but perhaps something interesting for our mother? She's shockingly difficult to buy for. Paul's conceded defeat."

Sally Summerfield had been a challenge, too, but I'd give anything to have her alive so I could agonize over the problem of suitable gifts for her. I let out a quiet sigh. "I wrote a thing about the craft sale for the local paper. The Coastal Courier. Very small deal, but it keeps people in touch."

"Paul has one on the coffee table. I'll have a look. And yes, our district at home has a local rag that we make fun of but never miss reading, so I know what you mean. Happy to visit Iona next." Heather waved a hand at our empty mug and cup. "On the house," she said softly, and we both grinned.

———

I SHOULD HAVE GONE HOME and attended to Elaine O'Blythe's latest tale about Kerry the kereru flapping around in the tree-ferns and kowhai trees, eating buds and flowers. But the weather was beautiful, Heather was easy company, and somehow I found we were ambling the length of Drizzle Bay's main street and checking out the shops. It's not a long main street at first glance, but the shops continue around the corner by Paul's church as far as the big old oak tree with the seat around it. Heaven only knows how that survives the salt spray.

"Good butcher," I said, indicating Bernie Karaka's meticulous display of steaks and cutlets and other meaty treats. "He and his wife adopted the two little dogs after Isobel died. And the Mini-mart's groceries cost a bit more than the big supermarket further north, but if you factor in the petrol to drive there, then it's not that much of a difference."

We walked a few steps further. "OMG! That's Mother to a T," Heather said, pointing to an out-of-season very sensible pink woolen cardigan with a collar. Yes, Drizzle Bay Modes is that kind of place, and I wasn't going to tell her I had exactly the same garment at home in jade green. No-one ever sees it except Graham, but when you're working at a keyboard for ages, something warm and cozy is just the ticket.

Then she gave a long, appreciative moan and stopped outside the Brides by Butterfly window next door. "That's just gorgeous," she whispered. "I had a great pouffy meringue of a wedding dress, but look at that slinky thing with the lacey fishtail. Pure Hollywood."

It was easy to picture her in it. Her pale skin and long blonde hair. Those innocent big blue eyes that hid all kinds of wicked twinkles. "Yes, I can definitely see you in that. To my mother's disappointment I chose a cream wool crepe suit and a hat with a veil."

Heather dragged her eyes away from the Hollywood dress and sent me a doubtful glance.

I shrugged. "I was past thirty and thought I looked suitably elegant, but the outfit was probably trying to tell me 'all downhill from here'."

"Don't," she said, giving me a nudge with an elbow. "I'm sure you looked very classy." Then she linked her arm through mine to slow me from walking any further until she'd had a good look at the rest of the wedding finery on display. "Brides by Butterfly," she murmured. "Nice name. Floaty and memorable – just like that dress over there."

"The owner's name is Buttercup," I said, trying not to laugh. "Belinda Buttercup. She could hardly have Brides by Buttercup because Buttercup sounds like a farmyard cow – not the least bit bridal."

"So she called the place Butterfly? Clever. Much more graceful and pretty." Heather peered into the window again and I let her look. We were just about to resume our wander when my phone exploded with 'Jingle Bells'. I scrabbled in my bag for it and found it was Bruce Carver. I could practically smell his cologne down the line.

"Good morning, Detective. Lovely day." (Or was that too chirpy?)

"Morning Ms Summerfield." By contrast he was sounding pretty abrasive. "Wondering if I could come around for that word. What time would suit?"

"I'm not at home. I'm out with Paul McCreagh's sister

who you saw last night. Just around the village, though. Not doing anything too important."

I'm sure I heard the cogs in his brain whirring before he said, "Two birds with one stone, then. Where can I meet you?"

I didn't fancy being grilled in a public place like Iona's café, so I suggested the side of St Agatha's church. There are a couple of big wooden benches there, set in an L shape, and partly in the shade of the pohutukawa trees. I'm sure he got the point we'd be away from flapping ears.

"Five minutes," he said. "I don't suppose you have Mr Jacobsen with you?"

Kill me now – I couldn't resist. "He's gone to buy another helicopter." I hoped that sounded as though I had friends who bought extra helicopters every day. "He won't be back for a while."

"Understood," Bruce Carver snapped. "I'll phone him."

And once again it seemed he was just around the corner because his car glided up and then stopped with a squeal only a couple of minutes later. Did he need new brake pads or something? Detective Marion Wick's very long legs slid out of the passenger side, followed by her equally slender body and over-large eyes.

"Wouldn't you like legs like those?" I muttered to Heather. This was possibly unfair because I hadn't seen Heather's legs out of trousers yet. Capris at the Burkeville for brunch, and camel-colored chinos today – no doubt chosen to be practical for our aerial jaunt. She could have amazing legs for all I knew.

I did the introductions. Marion Wick sat on the bench at an angle from Heather and me, and Bruce Carver seemed to feel more at home pacing up and down in front of us all – his harem of three. He wished.

He waited until Detective Wick had switched her phone to record and told it when and where and who. "Thank you for the Maisie Hardacre information last night," he began. "And for Mr Haldane's whereabouts. We'll investigate the old cottage and see if we can find him."

I took a deep breath, fearing the reaction that would surely follow. "When we flew over Devon Downs this morning –"

"This morning?" the DS barked. "What were you doing there?"

"Checking out suitable locations for a TV commercial. Have you been in contact with Graham today yet?"

There was a moment's silence. "Was he with you, too?"

"No, but I phoned him once we'd landed. He told me last night about Perce Percy having a new QE2 covenant over a big piece of his farm, and we saw someone was inside the fence because we spotted a stock truck partly hidden under a tree." I looked up to the leathery leaves and feathery tufts of scarlet flowers above me. "One of these. Quite large."

"And...?" That sounded as cold as ice cracking off a polar glacier.

"And I let Graham know, so he could check it out with Perce."

Marion Wick uncrossed her endless legs and leaned forward. "There certainly shouldn't be anyone there with a vehicle if the land is under covenant."

Heather cleared her throat. It seemed she'd conquered her giggles. "We didn't see people from the air. Only the truck."

I nodded along with her. "We wondered if it was the rustlers, and they'd put the meat in the car and also killed that boy, and were now hiding."

Bruce Carver looked daggers at me. "And why would you think that, Ms Summerfield?"

"Well...um...stock truck, rustling, keeping out of sight?"

I could see his teeth were clamped together. A sinew was jumping not far from his ear –presumably with fury at my impertinent theory.

Hoping to sweeten him up, I said, "I took some photos as we flew. We were doing it for possible filming locations, but there might be something useful for you?"

I never saw a man so desperate to get his hands on anything I possessed. Even Duncan Skeene on our wedding night hadn't looked so keen.

Oh, the twitching desire on poor Bruce's face as I scrolled to my shots from the helicopter and stood up to show him!

Marion Wick unfolded herself from the seat and moved to the other side of me, peering over my shoulder.

I was trapped. I couldn't breathe. The Carver cologne was

asphyxiating. I thrust my phone at him, stepped away, and sat down again, rummaging in my bag for anything I could sneeze into. Found a somewhat crumpled but clean-looking paper tissue – better than nothing. I held it to my nose, waiting for the tickle to turn explosive.

Heather's brows rose halfway to her hairline and she pressed her lips together. It looked like the giggles weren't far below the surface again.

Carver and Wick were in heaven. We may as well not have existed as they flicked to and fro, muttering to each other and pointing at things on the screen.

"Would you like to transfer some of those to your own phones?" I asked. "Then you can play with them any way you like. Print them out. Blow them up bigger. Whatever?"

Marion Wick sent me a distracted smile. DS Carver's gaze didn't lift.

She joggled his arm. "I'm still recording on mine, sir. Send them to yours."

He came out of his trance of concentration and looked across at her, blinking – rather like Graham does when I interrupt him at his office.

"Or shall I do it?" I offered, reaching forward and snagging my phone while trying to avoid his bitten fingernails. I wasn't too keen on the Police having free rein over *everything* in there.

"If you don't mind," he said. And then remembered his manners. "Thank you very much, Ms Summerfield."

So I did it, and returned my phone safely to my bag with

a slight sigh of relief. "All yours. Hope they're useful. Sorry I don't have any of the tree on the beach."

He shot me a glare of disbelief. "All taken care of yesterday by Mr Jacobsen and then the Scene of Crime team."

"Will you have to go up that farm track at the low end of the land?" I asked. "It looks like it'll be a bit bumpy."

The DS nodded and grimaced. "Yes, not a fun trip, but they obviously got the truck up that way. We'll use a four wheel drive. It doesn't quite merit the Police chopper, seeing no-one has reported another body."

I hoped I was only imagining an unspoken 'yet' on the end of his sentence.

10

WALKING INTO TROUBLE

AFTER SOME MORE QUESTIONS, which as far as I could see established nothing else useful, Carver and Wick drove away and Heather and I continued our stroll in the sun.

"Do you want five minutes in here?" I asked as we drew level with Winston Bamber's upmarket gallery.

She peered through the window at some big abstract panels. The surfaces appeared to undulate. I looked more closely and decided they'd been quilted or padded before being painted. Hadn't seen anything like them before. There were also striking driftwood-and-stone sculptures which reminded me of Nic who I'd met at the Horse Heaven crafting conference.

"It's beautiful stuff, but too big to get home easily," Heather said. "I'd love to look, though."

I reached for the big glass door to open it for her. "There might be smaller pieces at the craft sale," I murmured before we got close enough for Winston to overhear such sacrilege. "Cheaper, too."

She grinned and preceded me in to the light-filled space. Quiet classical music swirled in the rarified air.

Cravat-wearing Winston gave us about two minutes of peace before oozing out from his expensively appointed office and offering us his expertise. He's nice – I shouldn't describe him like that – but all the works have huge price tags and there are seldom any customers visible. Maybe he sells a lot online? There was speculation when Isobel Crombie died that she'd been helping him launder the proceeds from stolen artworks he was fencing. I've no idea how that would work. Mind you, Brett Royal was possibly people-smuggling on his whale watch boat, and Isobel herself was supplying cannabis grown in her large and very private garden to the Sand Knights motor cycle gang. Drizzle Bay is full of gossips, all desperate for a bit of excitement, and almost always wrong.

I waved an arm as though I was presenting a prize. "Winston, this is Vicar Paul McCreagh's sister, Heather."

"Visiting from England I'm afraid, so most of these lovely things will be far too big for my luggage," she said with a blink of her blue eyes and a pretty smile.

Winston stood a couple of inches taller and beamed at her, holding out a hand to shake. "We can easily arrange secure packaging and delivery across the world," he said. "Do it all the time."

She blinked again. "Certainly something to think about, then," she agreed.

I caught her slight wink and furtive grin in my direction. She was a lot flirtier than her brother! Paul is so gorgeously dependable and well-mannered he'd probably apologize if anyone thought he was flirting.

I tried to keep my expression neutral. "Heather's here for a break from the English winter."

"And I daresay you didn't expect to end up in the middle of a murder investigation," Winston suggested.

This time her eyes opened very wide. "I'm hardly in the middle," she protested.

He patted her hand, which he hadn't yet relinquished. "Goodness me, of course not. Not what I meant it all. But I gather you were in the helicopter when the body was discovered?"

Heather withdrew her hand and gave a dramatic shudder. Knowing her background I had no idea whether it was real or manufactured. "Terrible," she said. "Just terrible. So bizarrely laid out. I suppose the story has gone all around the village by now?"

Winston smiled, showing teeth so perfect they couldn't be real. "Not a lot of local news in a little place like this, so I'm afraid it was yesterday's hottest topic, and is still today's, no doubt."

"Midweek Murder," she muttered. "When I was younger I had a small part in a repertory production called that."

His carefully tamed salt-and-pepper brows rose over his

twinkling brown eyes. "You're an *actress*? What might I have seen you in?"

Heather was obviously used to being asked that because she rattled off a fast list that included 'a small part in Corry – tiny really – I was Geraldine in 'Tuscany Forever', the abused wife in 'You'd Never Suspect'... umm... the ditzy blonde housewife in a fish fingers campaign... but for the past several years I've been working on school productions – writing, producing, acting. No money in that, but enormous enjoyment."

"Young people have no qualms about making their honest views felt," Winston said. "I see parents in here wondering how to describe or appreciate something abstract and their child will bellow cheerfully, 'Dad – that looks like spew'."

I coughed a bit at that, but Heather simply grinned, and lisped, "Miss, Miss, I'm *not* kissing Brad Longfield." She changed to a brisk bossy tone. "You are if you want to play Juliet."

We both laughed, and moved off around the displays as a threesome. Winston still had the metallic striped timber tray I'd admired several times before. "Love that," I said to Heather, just as his phone rang. He excused himself to answer it, and we took the opportunity to walk somewhat faster. We reached the exit as he emerged from his office again.

"It's a fabulous gallery – I'll certainly be back," Heather

called as she opened the door and we made our escape to Iona's.

"So you're genuinely famous?" I asked.

She shook her head. "Had some nice parts – stage and TV, but no movies – because I didn't dare leave Rob alone for long as time went by." She narrowed her eyes at me. "*Don't* take that as sacrificing my life for his. I wouldn't have swapped a thing." She linked her arm through mine, and it felt like an apology for her sharp retort.

The tables outside Iona's resounded with cheerful chatter and the clink of cups on saucers and cake-forks on plates. Muffins and cupcakes and assorted other goodies glistened in the shafts of sunshine, bursting with raisins and blueberries, swirled with frosting, sprinkled with nuts and chocolate chips or cheese and bacon. No wonder the village boasted a few big tummies and stout legs these days! Heather peered with interest at some of the offerings.

"Morning Merry," our next door neighbor Nancy Simmons called as we drew near. She had her daughter Rochelle with her, but there was no sign of Kaydee-Jane so presumably the 'cold' had cleared up in time for the last few days of the school year.

"Morning Nancy," I said. She's a little dynamo of a woman and was a good friend to my mother.

"Excitement all over now?" she asked, no doubt referring to the leg of beef and Monday's visiting Police.

"A 'one-off', I'm sure."

"But then they found that body," Rochelle said, holding

the remains of a sausage roll aloft. Flakey pastry crumbs drifted down onto her ample lap.

"There's no guarantee they're connected," I said through slightly gritted teeth.

"And I heard the vicar's sister was there." Rochelle's eyes goggled in her pale face.

"Rochelle," I said in the sweetest tone I could manage, (which wasn't very sweet). "I'd like you to meet Vicar McCreagh's sister, Heather."

Nancy smirked. Rochelle crammed the rest of her sausage roll into her mouth and nodded like one of those parcel-shelf dogs that used to be popular in old cars.

"No – the helicopter pilot found it, if anyone did," Heather said. "I had the misfortune to be sitting beside him at that moment." She raised her hand, twiddled a few fingers in a parody of a wave. "Toodles," she said as she swept into the café, leaving Rochelle with chipmunk cheeks and Nancy trying to stop her smirk from growing wider.

Once we were clear of them, Heather leaned over and muttered in my ear, "Is this going to happen all day?"

"All week, I expect," I murmured back, trying to keep a straight face. "Good thing it's already Thursday."

We joined the end of Iona's short queue. She had an unknown girl behind the counter who appeared to be more of a hindrance than a help. I wondered if Heather would replace her if she proved useful, but no, she seemed keener on the actual baking than the shop aspect, so probably not. And she was only here for a while.

Beside me, she sighed. "It was better being the fish finger ditz. If this ends up on the news pages at home Mother will go full-fury."

I looked at her doubtfully. "Do you think it will?"

"Depends how much time and space they have to fill." She wrinkled her nose. "The internet has no size restrictions." She dialed down her volume. "English actress Heather Gregson, on an exotic holiday in coastal New Zealand, has been questioned by the Police after reporting a body on an isolated beach. Ms Gregson was enjoying a helicopter excursion with two handsome Americans.... No – make that 'two wealthy American entrepreneurs.' May as well make me sound as though I'm a gold-digger as well as the paramour of two men!"

I tried not to snort. Yes, I'd seen sensational reports like that for sure. High on excitement, low on facts.

She rolled her bottom lip in over her teeth while she thought for a moment longer. "Umm... Platinum blonde Ms Gregson will be remembered for her moving portrayal of the abused wife, Fiona, in the BBC's production of 'You'd Never Suspect'. Widowed only months ago, Ms Gregson fled to New Zealand to spend time with her war hero brother so she could heal in peace and privacy. It's rumored her mental state is now fragile'." She scowled. "And they'll dig out some terrible old publicity shot from a past production where I'm wearing a frizzy wig."

"You're not really 'platinum'," I objected.

"I'm a long way from 'fragile', too," she muttered.

I drew a breath. "Is Paul really a war hero?"

"In my eyes, for sure." Her sharp gaze dared me to think otherwise.

"Phone her," I suggested.

"We've already Skyped to prove I arrived safely."

I gave her a gentle dig with my elbow. "Yes, but this hadn't happened then. Get in first. Tell her how it really is now. And, by the way, you're good. I can see you doing a great commentary for the filming job."

She relaxed a little at my compliment. "It wouldn't be a bad idea to beat her to it. Might prevent her from hopping on the first available flight and trying to 'rescue' me."

"She wouldn't, would she?" I suddenly pictured Her Tweediness striding along the beach with a brace of hounds, hunting down her sorrowing daughter.

The customers immediately ahead of us uplifted their goodies and made their way to one of the indoor tables. Iona glanced behind us, decided the queue was now manageable, and said to the girl, "Michelle, you'll be okay on your own for a few minutes, won't you." It didn't look as though Michelle had any say in the matter.

Iona lifted a hinged section of the counter and beckoned us through to the kitchen. Heather stared around with unabashed interest until I introduced her. "Iona, this is Paul's sister, Heather Gregson. Heather, this is Iona Coppington."

"Strong family resemblance," Iona said, offering a hand to shake.

"You really think so?" I asked. Heather looked surprised and then added, "So pleased to meet you, Iona."

"Goodness yes," Iona said, tilting her inquisitive birdie face up to inspect Heather more closely. "Different coloring but the same long, elegant, English nose. Same set to the mouth."

"I don't like my nose much," Heather said.

"Not too fond of my chubby one, either," Iona chortled. "I'd rather have yours any day. Anyway... Merry says you're a keen baker?"

"Amateur only. I'd need direction, but I'm sure I could do anything you needed after that."

"Frosting? Icing? Birthday cakes for kids?"

Heather's eyes lit up. "Yes, anything fiddly or fancy I'm very good at."

"Christmas cakes?"

"Baking them or icing them?"

Iona looked sly. "Baked them months ago. They've been maturing, and getting a little drink of brandy now and then."

"Iona!" I exclaimed. "Are you allowed to do that without a liquor license?"

"I am sure it all evaporates," she said, not looking the least bit worried. "I could certainly do with some behind-the-scenes help for the next week or so."

They continued to chat, totally ignoring me.

"How about I nip home to change and come back for a trial run?" Heather suggested. "The rest of today, plus tomorrow to start with, and you can see if I'm useful."

"We'll have to work out how to pay you."

"I've been thinking about that. Could you make a contribution of Christmas cakes and Christmas puddings to Paul's big community lunch?"

"I'd be doing that anyway," Iona said, looking offended that Heather thought otherwise.

"Well, maybe a bit more than usual? I'd be perfectly happy with that. I'll be in heaven playing in here." She gazed around the spotless white kitchen with its stainless steel benches and commercial oven.

Iona shot her an assessing glare. "You won't consider it 'playing' if I throw three dozen cupcakes at you and ask for pointed clown hats, lemon drizzle icing, and a different expression on every face."

Heather rubbed her hands together and grinned. "Try me!"

"All done in half an hour."

"Ah. I'll speed up with practice."

"I can see you two are going to get on *fine*," I said to Iona, hitching my bag more firmly over my shoulder. "We had no breakfast because we were going up in a helicopter, so maybe we could grab coffee and a muffin and then I'll leave you to it."

"Back to your lonely laptop?" Heather suggested.

"Not so lonely this time. It's my favorite author – the one who does her own animal paintings."

"Elaine O'Blythe?" Iona demanded, her face tilted to one side like an inquisitive budgie. "Has she got a new book coming out? Will it be in time for my youngest grandies for Christmas?"

I shook my head. "Bit of work to do yet."

She sighed. "They've got all the others. They love them. I still need to buy a few bits and pieces for them."

"Come to the craft sale at Horse Heaven with us?" I suggested. "We thought we'd have a look on Sunday."

"Ummm..." Heather said. "What time? I said I'd help Paul with a Sunday School nativity rehearsal mid-morning before he does the Family Service. An item to perform at the community lunch."

I clapped a hand to my chest. "Sorry. Should have thought."

"Two o'clock?" Iona suggested, and we both nodded.

———

LIFE WENT BACK to normal for the next couple of days, and with no murder progress to distract me, I got plenty of editing work done. Then, after lunch on Sunday, the three of us bundled into the Focus and made our way to Old Bay Road. Horse Heaven baked under the summer sun. Plums and apricots glowed from among the leaves of Betty McGyver's trees. The same horse who'd escorted me last time trotted up the driveway beside us on the other side of the fence again, whickering a soft welcome.

"Isn't he *beautiful!*" Heather exclaimed from the back seat.

I could easily imagine her in jodhpurs and a riding helmet, cantering around the Derbyshire countryside.

Parking was at quite a premium once we got closer to the big barn, but I squeezed us into a gap someone else was vacating. It looked like the ladies were having a very successful sale.

And so it proved. Betty was beside herself with glee. "Merry," she enthused. "Such a great turn-out. Thank you so much for getting that item into the Coastal Courier for us. And they used both of the photos."

"Not surprised," I said as we all turned toward the barn. "You set the goodies up to look so pretty for them."

Some time ago I'd come out to Horse Heaven to what was loosely described as a crafting conference. I'd been following a hunch about the Isobel Crombie murder, and farmer Betty had been kind enough to feed me brunch (delicious bacon from a much-loved pig previously known as Harold). "You'll remember Iona from the café, of course," I said, recovering my manners. "And this is Heather, Vicar Paul's sister."

"Here for a Kiwi summer," Heather said, shaking Betty's proffered hand.

"Can we chat for a minute?" Betty asked, politely making it plain she wanted me but not Iona or Heather. I waved them to go on ahead of me, and Betty led me between two parked cars. "This murder," she said, as soon as we couldn't be overheard. "Any progress yet?"

Why would Betty be so desperate to know? I must have looked at her rather sharply because she followed up with,

"I'm on my own here at night. If anyone decides to steal my stock they'll get a blast up their backsides from my shotgun."

"Fair enough, too," I agreed. "But that quarter-cow in our garage was either from Drizzle Farm or Devon Downs, so I don't think you need to worry too much over this side of the bay."

"They've narrowed it down to those two properties?"

"Yes, but that's confidential for now. Okay?"

She nodded, looking somewhat less on edge. "Good to know. So they're making progress. Anyone in mind for the murder?"

"Not yet, as far as I know, although why would Bruce Carver tell me?" I leaned closer to her. "He had a word with both Heather and me this morning but he wasn't giving anything away."

Betty had to be content with that. I wasn't getting into speculation. There was plenty of that swirling around the village already.

Heather, Iona and I spent a happy hour or so wandering around the stalls and eventually departed with a hand-crocheted merino infinity scarf for Heather and Paul's mother, and three pairs of earrings and a patchwork bag created from varying shades of old denim jeans for me. Iona chose hand-knitted glove puppets with ping pong ball heads and huge smiles for her younger grandchildren, and half a dozen very ugly mini-zombie dolls made from wooden clothes pegs, which she declared would be perfect stocking-fillers for her twelve year old twin grand-daughters.

"Zombie cupcakes?" Heather suggested as we walked back to the car. "Gray frosting, big frightened eyes, a trickle of blood?" She and Iona fell about laughing.

"Hmmm... school holidays," I said. "They might even be worth a try."

"Totally," Heather agreed. "Can't be more gruesome than Evie Garrison's attempt at being the Virgin Mary in this morning's nativity rehearsal. Her older sister did her makeup. She made her look like some sort of rock-star – Alice Cooper, or the blokes from Kiss – black-rimmed eyes and skin as white as a geisha."

"Or a panda?" Iona suggested, and we all dissolved into laughter again.

I should probably admit we'd tried some samples of fruit wines – Heather and Iona much more than me, seeing I was driving. The hilarity was probably out of proportion to the topic. The supply of the wine was possibly not legal. On private property? Given away and not sold? Who cared – they were surprisingly nice wines on a gorgeous summer day and we were feeling no pain.

I beeped the car unlocked. "Is this okay on the seat beside you?" I asked Heather, handing her my new patch-work denim bag with the rest of the things inside it. She'd insisted chubby Iona sat in the front on the way here, and was already climbing into the back again.

"No worries – where's my card from that wine-maker?" she asked, fumbling around her pockets. "I'm definitely going to order a box of the elderflower champagne. And some of that raspberry gin."

There'd been gin? I hadn't seen that, and maybe just as well!

Right as she located the card, my phone burst into 'Jingle Bells'. John's name appeared on the screen and his deep voice rumbled into my ear. "I'm taking the dogs for a run out past the Point. Wondered if you wanted to come for a beach walk on such a nice day?"

My skin prickled, thinking of that kiss. Was this really just an invitation for a walk? I wouldn't bring the spaniels, in case.

11

MAN-HANDLED

BRINGING – or not bringing – the spaniels made no difference as it happened.

John collected me in the black pick-up with Fire and Ice secured in the tray. "Are they okay?" I asked, peering around at their big faces looking at us through the rear window.

"They're working dogs, not pets," he said. "Lick you to death if they were in the back seat."

Euw – they had very big mouths with huge, long tongues!

Taking very little notice of the speed limit, he roared down Drizzle Bay Road. "So you're playing the Mom in the commercial and the vicar's being the Dad?"

"Only from the back," I said. "And hardly 'playing'. We'll just be bodies the right size and age."

"I'll be shooting you. Could sneak your face in, if you want?"

"*You'll* be shooting us?"

"Did quite a lot of video surveillance in the past. Comes in handy..."

Hmmm. The Black Ops rumors floated to the top of the murky things I knew (or maybe didn't know) about him. "Have you worked all over the world?"

"Nowhere as peaceful as this," he said, which didn't tell me much.

"War zones?"

"Yup."

I waited for anything else. It wasn't forthcoming. "And?"

"Industrial espionage. People who need watching." He shrugged, and sent me a lazy grin. "Not always a nice world out there."

"So you're here for some peace and quiet?"

"Here for whatever turns up."

He was infuriating! I couldn't tell if he was doing it on purpose or not. He wasn't actually rude but he was way less than forthcoming.

After a few more minutes he pulled into the space by the beach access path. This was where I'd first seen his truck all those weeks ago. The cottage was only about a hundred yards away, but the big white X of the tree trunk had to be further on because the wheel-tracks we'd seen from the air led to Drizzle Farm's land. I'd be keeping clear of that, for sure.

"So here we are," John said. "I'll only be half an hour."

As Fire and Ice and John bounded off into the distance I gave them half a wave they never saw and started to amble along the tangled strip of seaweed and shells, wondering what treasures I might discover. So far it seemed the invitation really had been for a walk – and a walk on my own, at that.

I picked up a long, smooth stick and used it to poke at some of the thicker clumps of seaweed and kelp. Found a really big paua shell, gleaming blue and turquoise and violet. Then a much smaller, paler one. It was a little honey so I gave it a rub and slipped it into my pocket. This was followed by the most amazing convoluted piece of driftwood. I easily pictured our mother using that in one of her rather creative flower arrangements. Not being a floral artist myself I left it behind and wandered on, thinking fond thoughts of her.

The air smelled super salty. The breakers thundered in under the lowering sun, tossing plumes of spray behind them as they raced toward the shore. I was surprised John was running instead of surfing. He was good to the Shepherds though. Fire and Ice were pictures of health – thick shiny coats, bright dark eyes, and bursting with energy. They ran faster than him, and he was going at a fair clip. The dogs easily outpaced him and then circled back to start the race again, kicking up sand and barking joyfully.

I watched as they moved further and further away and then returned to my slow beachcombing. Found a strange flat shell the like of which I'd never seen before. When you grow up beside the ocean there's not much you don't recognize. Maybe this had been washed up from somewhere very deep? I slid that into my pocket beside the little paua shell.

I was in a deeply peaceful place when I heard an urgent shriek of, "Help, please!" from somewhere behind me. I whipped around – on edge to suddenly have company. At least it was a woman's voice, although plainly a panicked one. I was amazed to find it was Margaret Alsop.

She'd looked bad at the Burkeville on Wednesday – the day Paul and I had taken Heather to brunch there, and Margaret had called in to buy a croissant, intending to share it with Pierre the poodle. Now she looked absolutely terrible. She appeared to have aged another ten years. Her peroxided hair was scraped back into an untidy ponytail and her big bosom was at least all covered this time, but the stretchy top she wore did nothing to disguise its dimensions.

"Margaret!" I stared at her. She'd scrambled down onto the beach from the old cottage's garden. She was panting hard and pink in the face under her unnatural yellow-blonde hair. It was a real shock to see her.

"I thought it looked like you," she gabbled. "I hoped it was. Can you help? This is urgent. This is *really* urgent." At that moment there was a loud masculine yell and two angry men came barreling over the highest sand hill, heading straight in our direction.

"Oh God!" she gasped. "It's them. They're home early."

My mouth must have been a total 'O' of surprise. I didn't expect she'd be so destitute she'd need to take in lodgers to make ends meet.

"Three of them," she quavered. "Demanding to stay here because it's out of sight. Two nasty big dogs as well. Pierre is terrified of them, and they keep threatening to feed him to them if I don't do what they want."

I stared across at the two men who were making as much haste as they could, stumbling through the low beachy scrub. They'd be all over us in thirty seconds.

Three men, two dogs. Could they be the rustlers from the green stock truck? The intruders DS Carver had evicted from Perce Percy's land? Was this where they'd disappeared to?

I twisted away in the hope they couldn't see what I was doing and grabbed my cell phone. Tapped out the fastest text in the world to John. *3 men 2 dogs cottage get help.* And attempted to stuff the phone back in my pocket, hoping they hadn't seen me sending it. Fat chance, of course.

"You can forget that, Blondie," the first of them said, slinging an arm around my neck in a chokehold and diving for the phone with his other hand. He wrenched it out of my fingers and hurled it into the sea.

Noooo.... all my contacts! What a stupid thought – I should have been thinking 'all my oxygen' but the human brain is a very strange thing.

"Aaaarrgghhh..." was all I could manage, and Margaret sounded a lot the same. The two men forced us back up the beach, an arm across a throat, the other around a waist, turning and dragging us when we couldn't manage to walk properly in their tight grips. They were big and tough and smelly – unpleasantly perfumed with old perspiration, beery breath and animal dung. The one forcing me along had rough, calloused hands and horribly scratchy whiskers that kept digging into the side of my face. He'd clamped a punishing fist around my jaw. I would have loved to bite him but had no chance to.

In the far, far, far distance I glimpsed John wheeling around and stopping. I prayed he was grabbing his phone from the pouch on his arm and reading my text. Was there even reception that far along the beach? Would he be able to call the Police?

To my consternation he set off running again – straight back in our direction. The only good thing happening here was that the men had to watch their step through the pieces of driftwood and tufts of rough sand tussock and low whippy branches of coprosma that would have tripped us and had us off our feet in an instant. With any luck they hadn't seen John, and anyway why would they take much notice of a solo half-clad runner out exercising his dogs?

I tried to dig my heels in and be as annoying as possible for the beast who was hauling me along, but that only earned me a tug on my hair and a loud growl of, "Walk or I'll slap you one!" I had no doubt he'd carry through on that gruff threat. I glanced sideways at Margaret. She was smaller than me and a good twenty years older so was no doubt easier to drag. The barbarian holding her was groping a breast with a big hand. Her eyes were scrunched closed. If I ever got the chance, I'd squeeze something of his in return. Tightly. With no mercy at all.

I flicked my gaze back along the beach. John and the dogs

were pounding along at equal speed now so he must have picked up his pace enormously.

Stay away, stay away, I prayed, and was relieved to see him veer gradually down the sand until he was running at the very edge of the tide. The sun sparkled on the water drops he and the dogs kicked up. Just a sporty chap out for a run, and keeping well clear; that was all our captors would see if they took any notice of him at all.

They'd now dragged us most of the way up the incline leading to the old cottage garden. Margaret and I were both panting and groaning out our displeasure, and this earned me the threatened slap on the side of my head. I saw stars for a few seconds but was grateful it was a slap and not a punch.

At last we reached level ground. The man who'd been hauling me along changed his grip so he had a big handful of my hair instead of my throat. It was an enormous relief. "Walk," he demanded, pushing me forward across the expanse of grass that was too rough to properly be called a lawn. The man dragging Margaret was only a couple of steps behind.

"What are you going to do to us?" I begged.

"Wait and see," he ground out. "I hope you can cook better than the old girl."

"What?"

'Don't say 'what', darling,' my dear departed mother inserted.

"They've stayed the last couple of nights," Margaret gasped in my direction, probably incensed and given bravery by that unflattering description. "They've brought lots of meat."

I immediately thought of the huge haunch of beef that had been left in Graham's car. Were they in possession of the other three quarters? Surely not. It would be stinking rotten by now, although then I thought about how delicious Bernie the butcher's steaks were when they were well hung. Maybe they'd got it into a chiller in good time?

Trust me to be thinking about food at such a moment!

Now it was easier to walk, my captor had me by my hair and the waistband of my jeans. I rubbed at my abused throat and at the side of my face where I'd been slapped. "You okay?" I called across to Margaret.

"Don't worry about Grandma." That grated right into my ear.

"Not really," she quavered. "They did something to the car so I couldn't get away. And took my phone."

I thought of the old-fashioned landline, almost hidden behind a curtain in the hallway. Had they seen that too?

"And the old one in the hall," she added. "Tore it right out of the wall."

I could absolutely see why she'd been traumatized. In just a few months her life had totally turned to custard. Her sister had been murdered. The man she'd presumably loved was charged with serious auto theft crimes and jailed. She'd lost her beautiful house and swanky car, and been reduced to staying in the dilapidated old beach cottage where her parents had lived for many years. And now this.

Then deep barking echoed across to us, although no dogs were yet in sight. They sounded like big rough dogs. Probably used for hunting. And guard duty on this occasion. I hoped little white Pierre was still safe.

We were hauled around to the side of the cottage and I truly expected the dogs to rush across and attack us, but the third man – on dog-feeding duty to judge by his bloodied hands – gave a sharp whistle and bellowed, "Stay!" To my great relief there was a clanking of chains, and they returned to gnawing at some big bony remnants of carcass by the fence. They were huge, rangy dogs – a good match for the men. Tall and fit and very hairy. Even after all my dog-walking duties for the Drizzle Bay Animal Shelter I couldn't hazard a guess as to what breed, or indeed mixture of breeds, they were. Horrible things, and rather smelly.

Even though it was a warm day, I shivered. How scary it must have been for poor Margaret here on her own and bailed up by such a team. How brave she'd have needed to be to survive unscathed. Presumably she'd caught a glimpse of me on the lonely beach from one of the cottage windows and decided to take her chances.

But how long before John could get the Police back here? From his steady progress out in the shallows he was a man on a mission and had definitely read my message.

"Good – you got 'er," the dog-feeder grunted. "And a little friend," he added, inspecting me with far-too-interested eyes.

At that moment I knew what true fear was. We were way out of sight and hearing of any other humans. Three of them to two of us. Two big dogs versus poodle Pierre. "Tie 'em up for now," he added, dragging a couple of outdoor chairs away from the side of the house and setting them back to back. Margaret and I were pushed down into them, which caused our heads to crack together hard enough to make us both squawk with pain.

"Sorry," I gasped, as though it had been my fault.

"It's okay," she muttered. "You still all right?"

"Took her phone," 'my' man said with an evil laugh. "Chucked it in the sea."

The third man headed across to the pickup truck we'd seen from the air on Wednesday. Plainly not a lawn mowing contractor. From ground level it was obvious they'd parked it so it was out of sight of the road, maybe to do a recce of the area. He grabbed a big coil of rope, then changed his mind and chose instead a much shorter piece and tossed it across. "Round their necks and through the chair arms," he grated. "They won't be going anywhere roped together like that. Hold'em for now, anyway."

Seconds later we were trussed together in a two-woman, two-chair bundle and certainly couldn't manage even a slow shuffle.

The dogs were now making horrible cracking noises as they crunched at the bones. It was too easy to imagine being their next meal.

"Beer?" one of the men called. I presumed he wasn't aiming that at Margaret or me, although I could have murdered one about now. Or a wine. Or even a glass of water.

My mouth was dry with fear. I licked my lips, unable to push my hair out of my eyes because of the way the rope had been laced around my wrists and the chair arms. It was horrible rough rope, all frayed and fibrous. It hurt. I was afraid I'd bash into Margaret again if I tried to toss my head sideways so I sat there in absolute misery, half blinded and wondering what they had planned for us. Cookery seemed the least of it.

"I always felt safe here when I was looking after Itsy and Fluffy," I muttered to Margaret as our three captors disappeared inside the cottage to enjoy their drinks.

"Me too, until this lot turned up."

"They haven't... interfered with you?" I asked, wondering if that was a delicate enough description for an older lady.

"No, thank goodness," she murmured. "So far they seem to want to stay out of sight and be fed. They smoke a lot of what they call 'weed'."

Huh! Was it their marijuana up in the pine plantation? Maybe they really had killed Beefy junior to keep him away from it. But why would they draw attention to him by putting him on display on that big X of a tree? Unless of course they were high as kites and it simply seemed like a good idea at the time...

We sat there unspeaking after that, my mind going a million miles an hour. Fifty yards away the waves crashed over and rushed up the shore. Much nearer, the dogs gnawed and cracked their dinner apart. Rough male conversation floated out through the open doorway from the kitchen.

Then, through the curtain of my hair, I sensed a shape. A

tall, silent, shirtless shape. I did my best to flick my hair aside without hurting Margaret, and stared in disbelief at John. He was creeping closer with his arms full of 'something'. I opened my mouth and he gave one sharp shake of his head. Fire and Ice were stalking along just behind him, on feet as quiet and sure as their master's.

One of the hairy hounds suddenly raised its head from the gory carcass remains and gave a 'wuff' of warning. Fire and Ice both growled low in their throats.

"They're chained!" I blurted as John sprinted past them and stationed himself behind the big clump of hollyhocks by the door.

A storm of barking and chain-rattling rent the peaceful air and I felt Margaret lurching around in her chair, trying to see what was happening. "Keep still and low," I hissed, and I shrank down to make myself the smallest possible target.

Curses and loud grumbles about the 'effing dogs' floated through the doorway, followed by heavy footsteps. One of the men lurched outside, beer can in hand. John stuck out a foot, and man and beer hit the concrete, followed almost instantly by John, who grabbed a handful of unkempt hair and banged the head it was attached to once more on the hard surface. The man stayed down, stunned at the very least. All four dogs were now having a gigantic bark-off.

"Gordy?" a second man bellowed from inside the house. When he received no reply he sauntered to the door, took a couple of steps forward, kicked the fallen man's ankle none too gently, and yelled back at his mate, "Drunk as a skunk.

Fell over." Then he stared across at the dogs and saw Fire and Ice – focused, rumbling with threats, and keeping just out of reach. "Rifle," he yelled, the same instant as John leaped from cover and repeated the trip-and-head-smack treatment.

But 'rifle'?

My blood ran cold. Had the third man heard over the barking? Would he come out shooting? John's reaction was to dive inside the house, crouching low, before anyone else appeared. My heart galloped behind my ribs – a frantic, erratic tattoo. The slice of ham quiche I'd enjoyed at the craft sale threatened to re-appear, and I held my breath in case that helped it stay put. The now empty beer can trundled noisily over the concrete as the sea breeze caught it.

Nooooo..... John couldn't possibly take down a man with a rifle when he was dressed for a run on the beach. I squeezed my eyes closed, willed my ears to capture any hopeful progress over the cacophony the dogs were making, and prayed quite hard, although I'm not a very religious woman.

Thirty seconds later John appeared.

Dragging the third man by the ankles. He was even limper than his mates.

Fire and Ice got told to 'shut it' and reverted to low growls.

"What's happening?" Margaret quavered from behind me.

"John got all three of them," I yelled jubilantly over the remaining barking. Margaret burst into hiccupping tears.

I have to admit John was panting a bit. His broad chest rose and fell faster than usual, and the abs on his long, lean torso were flexing in and out. He piled the third man close to his groggy mates and stood still for a moment watching them, legs braced, hands clenching and unclenching, jaw tight. "Get to you two in a minute," he said to me, slashing a vicious-looking knife through part of the rope holding me captive and then moving swiftly to retrieve whatever it was he'd been carrying when he arrived.

He spread out a huge net as I tackled the rope. Who goes running with a huge net?

Then he dragged each of the cursing, struggling men onto it, pinching something in their necks to knock any further fight out of them, pulled the sides of the net over, and they were soon as neatly trussed as flies in a spider's web.

"Doing okay ladies?" he asked, unlashing the rest of the rope holding us to the chairs. Margaret and I managed shocked nods and murmurs of 'Mmm' as he flicked the ends apart and set us free. We both gazed at the pile of stunned, tangled-up men as John bent over them, threaded 'our' rope through some of the holes in the net, and yanked it tight. He tied a much better knot than our captor had; there was no way they could possibly escape now.

Even the dogs sensed they were beaten. They retreated to the fence and flopped down beside the remains of their bony dinner.

I rose from the chair very slowly, ignoring the groans and profanities coming from the bodies inside the net. I was shocked for sure. How had he done it?

"You wonderful man!" Margaret gushed, flinging herself against John and giving him an enthusiastic and bosomy bear-hug. He looped his arms around her in return, patting her shoulder until he could disentangle himself.

I pointed straight at him while she couldn't see me. "Black Ops," I mouthed. Then I said out loud, "I didn't believe it until now, but after seeing that..."

John shook his head. "Not me."

I shook mine in turn. "Yeah, right."

We grinned at each other like a pair of conspirators.

"So how did you produce this handy net out of thin air?" I asked, aiming a hard kick at the backside of the man who'd been squeezing Margaret's boob. He gave an enraged bellow and a loud curse. If he'd been the other way up I'd have kicked him somewhere a lot more painful. Oh well, you do what you can.

Margaret finally let go of John and sat down on one of the chairs again.

"Piece of good luck," John said. "I collected it earlier from someone who was into deer recovery. Erik wanted a sling to transport kayaks for some of my survival treks. It was in the tray of the truck.

I shook my head. "So without that we'd still be waiting for the Police?"

"No way!" He looked mortally offended, and then

glanced across to where Fire and Ice sat, waiting for their next orders. "I'd have given them one each to guard and I'd have looked after the third." He seemed to have no doubt it was possible.

Huh. Well. Okay then.

"I'll go and check on Pierre," Margaret said, rising and tottering into the house.

I took a deep breath and sat down again, knees nowhere near steady yet. "Thank you. Thank you for picking up the text. And for coming to the rescue in such spectacular fashion."

John narrowed his eyes and then looked down at the three men. "Time they got stopped," he said. "Carver and Wick knew about the pot-growing, and I'm sure they have their suspicions about young Haldane's death, even if no proof yet. But this is concrete; kidnapping two women will do nicely to get them out of circulation for a while." He rubbed a hand over my shoulder. Warm. Steady. I almost tilted my head and laid my cheek against it.

12

FLYING HIGH

"I WASN'T *EXACTLY* KIDNAPPED," I protested.

"Not the way I saw it," John said, turning to listen as tires screamed around the bend by Drizzle Farm and some absolutely disgusting curses issued forth from the men on the ground.

"Nice to hear Carver's lot putting some effort in," he added as the accelerating vehicles roared closer.

I pulled a rueful face. "They'll be getting sick of me."

He grinned. "You're giving them more fun than they've had in ages. A change from shoplifters and drunk drivers."

"A quarter of a cow and now three men in a net. That's definitely different." I gave in to a fit of nervous giggles and John let loose a bellow of deep laughter.

"How'd you know about the effing cow?" a rough voice grated from the tangle of bodies.

"You put it in the wrong car." I really enjoyed passing that on.

"Jeez, Gordy..."

"Brand new silver-gray Merc. Followed him all the way." Presumably that was Gordy trying to justify himself.

The first of the Police vehicles squealed to a halt and drowned any other comments. The two young officers who'd kindly removed the beef from Graham's trunk came barreling onto the driveway and stopped dead.

John gave a sharp whistle and called, "Truck!" Fire and Ice gave one last growl in the direction of the rustlers' dogs and raced away, presumably to the black pick-up out of sight along the road. "Those two are chained up," he said, jerking his chin at the big hunting dogs and their well-gnawed bones.

"And these three are *tied* up," I added. "Mrs Alsop is inside the cottage with her poodle."

"All under control then," one of the officers said, looking over his shoulder as the next car braked to a stop and the doors flew open. "How are we going to find their hands to get the cuffs on?"

Not my problem," John said. "I caught them. You cuff them. Or we could dump the whole bundle on the tray of my truck and untangle them once you have them somewhere secure?"

I could tell he was joking, but the younger of the policemen seemed to be considering it. Another storm of obscenities rose from the trio in the net.

John raised enquiring brows over wicked blue eyes. "Shame. Might have been fun." He turned and gave the cops half a salute. "When Carver wants me, he knows where to find me." And he strode away.

"I'll be there in a minute," I yelled after him, watching his long tanned legs eating up the ground until he'd disappeared. "I'll make sure Mrs Alsop is okay," I said in the direction of the policemen. I wanted to be nowhere near those men once they were untied.

John was waiting for me when I emerged from checking on Margaret. He'd driven back from the beach access path to save me the short walk in my shocked and shaky state, and looked thoroughly apologetic. "Not what I had in mind," he said. "Just thought it was a great day to enjoy the ocean."

I attempted a smile. My whole face felt trembly. "I need to buy a new phone. Mine got thrown in to the water when they saw me texting you."

His piercing blue eyes narrowed and his lips pressed together briefly before he said, "Honey, I'm sorry. Let me pay for it."

I stared at him, amazed he'd even think of offering. "But you rescued us. You don't owe me a thing. I'll check with my insurance company."

"Not quite how I feel about it," John muttered. "If I hadn't brought you here you wouldn't have been grabbed or lost your phone."

"And poor old Margaret would still be stuck in the cottage with *them*, scared stiff," I pointed out.

He hitched a shoulder in an apologetic shrug. "If you call your provider they should be able to transfer your account over pretty fast. You want me to take you to buy a new one tomorrow?"

———

Of course John knew 'someone in the business' who could give me a deal. Monday flew by in a flash, and with the TV shooting approaching fast, so did Tuesday.

Graham was just about beside himself with worry and protectiveness after the recent action and danger. He phoned me from the office much more often than usual, making sure I was safe, that I had the door locked if I was working, that I didn't need him to come home and provide company. Honestly, he was as clucky as an old hen. He was a jolly nuisance sometimes, interrupting my concentration as I was trying to unscramble Elaine O'Blythe's manuscript with the help of her delicate watercolors. But... yes... it's nice to be thought about so I tried not to snap at him. I may have rolled my eyes quite a lot while he couldn't see my face.

Wednesday dawned bright and clear. The excitement level for some of us was ramped up to ridiculous as we milled around in front of Kirkpatrick's barn. Both helicopters gleamed in the sun. Presumably someone had polished the Squirrel for its starring role because it looked amazing. Even so, I caught Erik rubbing his elbow on something that was possibly a tiny smear.

Heather was her composed self, a clipboard tucked into the crook of her elbow, and her hair in a gorgeous French twist up-do. Ten Ton Smedley looked like a double-size Tom Cruise in his Top Gun gear. Well, maybe it was his mechanic's overalls, but with aviator sunglasses he seemed pretty cool to me. He was obviously itching to leave the ground. John and Erik were as chill as ever, but Bailey, Pete and Mac resisted all of Lisa's efforts to calm them down.

"You're in charge of them," she muttered to me out of Ten Ton's hearing.

"He's their dad," I protested.

"He's flying John and that'll keep him plenty occupied. He's got the bag with the kids' spare clothes. Because of his size, no other passenger today."

Paul and I looked at each other doubtfully. What had we got ourselves into? I had indeed squeezed myself into the dreaded Spanx before hauling on my best dark jeans and a wine red blouse. He – no doubt also at Heather's instruction – wore khaki shorts and an oatmeal-colored T-shirt. With any luck I'd disappear into the shadows and he'd look like a plant hunter from the tropics with his very good legs and tousled dark hair.

I peered at him more closely. Although there was a light breeze, not a hair moved. I suspected Heather had taken to him with some sort of 'product'. The effect was *tres sexy*.

"I like what she's done to your hair."

"Stiff as concrete," Paul muttered, tapping a cautious

finger against an artful lock that had been arranged to droop over his brow.

"Very Hugh Grant."

His big brown eyes shot wide open. "Really?"

"I've always thought there were similarities."

He sent me a shy smile. "Both English," was all he said, but the pleased grin hovered around for quite a while.

I waited for Erik to yell something like 'Listen up, people!' like they do in movies, but instead it was Heather who reached into Paul's car, gave a loud blast on the horn, and waited for silence.

"Right," she announced. "Paul, Merry, Erik and the children into the Squirrel with me please. John will shoot us taking off, flying low, flying higher. Then he and Ten will follow and overtake so they can shoot us landing." She slammed the car door. "Can you lock this, Paul?"

Obediently he reached into the pocket of his shorts and found the key-ring with the remote. The car beeped and flashed.

Off we went. The new machine was definitely a step up from the other one, and now I knew a little more about what to expect I enjoyed the views enormously. Erik flew straight along Drizzle Bay Road. "Look down there," I said, pointing out the vet clinic to Bailey, Pete and Mac. I suspect they were way ahead of me, but they politely indulged 'Mum's friend' with smiles and nods. The harnesses at least kept them confined in their seats.

"Drizzle Farm," I said, spotting the glittering gateposts Alex had decorated. I hadn't done our loquat tree out the front yet – maybe later today?

"Devon Downs," Erik informed us all a minute or two later. "So we're going up over this range of hills and then you'll see the conservation area."

We soared on, following the smaller machine and waiting until it had landed. "No smoke today," I said for Erik's benefit. The vegetation stretched green and peaceful down to the stream.

"No truck either," he said when we reached the big flowering pohutukawa. "Looks like the Police have removed it."

Ten Ton had set John down well to one side of the big flat area, and his camera was already mounted on a tripod as Erik eased the Squirrel to the ground as gently as a bee settling on a flower. The children needed no encouragement to race around looking as though they were having an excellent time. A little more coaxing was required before they agreed to hide in the trees and change into their swimming gear, but soon they were all splashing energetically with the cascading waterfall as a fantastic backdrop. Paul and I were expected to stand to one side, holding hands like a happily married couple keeping an indulgent eye on 'our' offspring.

He continued the warm grip even when I was sure it was no longer necessary, but then Heather called out, "Lay your head on his shoulder, Merry."

I'd never laid my head on anyone's shoulder while out on

a picnic with children, but it was no hardship to stand there in the sun leaning on a handsome man. Paul let go of my hand and wrapped his arm around my waist as we stood together waiting to be instructed to break apart. Heather must have forgotten us because no instruction ever came.

Instead, a picnic hamper of the Burkeville's best treats appeared, and John shot close-ups of Mac biting into an over-filled croissant, Pete rolling his eyes with glee as he pulled a strip of bacon from a big slice of quiche, and Bailey licking the frosting from a strawberry cupcake as though she was a fastidious kitten. The cupcake looked to me as though it had come straight from Iona's kitchen. I raised an eyebrow at Heather and she winked back. Maybe she was drumming up trade for her new boss?

"Prettier than a muffin," she murmured, handing around bottles of water. We all joined in the feast and I was amazed to find it was already well after midday.

"So that just leaves some 'straight to camera' pieces from me," she said, consulting her clip-board after we'd eaten. She glanced at the sky. "We could do them another day because those clouds are going to be over the sun in a few minutes."

We all squinted up. Sure enough it looked as though the weather was changing fast. The clouds were thickening and changing from fluffy white to threatening bruise-like hues.

"You warm enough, kids?" Ten Ton asked. "Mum packed towels and fleeces in the bag."

Little Pete gave a theatrical shiver. "It's getting colder."

"I'll grab it," Paul said, bouncing to his feet and jogging across to the smaller machine. By the time he returned Heather had the picnic leftovers stowed and the air was definitely chilly. It was growing darker, and all around us the trees exuded quiet menace. Then I realized the birds had stopped singing. "Feels like thunder, maybe?" I said.

"Noooo..." Bailey wailed. "I hate thunder."

"Of course it won't," Ten Ton rumbled. But I saw him looking up at the sky, and I also saw him and Erik both cocking their heads and listening intently. John had packed his camera and tripod away and was already standing.

Then we heard the first gunshot – the sharp explosion and the eerie whistling through the air.

"Ten – take the kids and GO!" John yelled. Ten Ton raced his tribe of three across the rough ground, practically threw them in, slammed the door, and swung himself up into the pilot's seat. It seemed an age before we heard the blades start their slow thumping rotation but I suppose it's not like switching on a car engine. Meantime we were grabbing anything we could and diving toward the other machine as shots grew louder and nearer, and spatters of rain started to fall.

Something large crashed through the trees, making no effort at stealth. It grew nearer and nearer, screaming incoherently. Definitely human, which was probably a relief; at least no previously undiscovered dinosaur or hairy yeti was going to attack us. I might have heard a second voice as we slammed our door.

I guess clear windows are no great protection, but anything... anything... between us and what was out there was good. My heart tried to thump out of my chest and I found my hands were freezing when I wrapped them across myself for comfort. They say all the blood leaves your extremities and races to your vital organs when fear kicks in. Fear had certainly kicked. Hard. No doubt my feet and nose and ears were icy too.

"Going to be nasty," Erik grated, and we held on to each other as he alternately coaxed and swore at the Squirrel until it was a roaring live thing, lifting off with a lurch that had Heather and me gasping. He immediately spun the machine to present a smaller target to whoever was shooting.

We'd gained only a few meters of height when the first shot thwacked one of the skids. Then the second. I'd rather the skid than the cabin, but this was way too close for comfort. I wanted to vomit up my pounding heart.

"Asshole!" Erik yelled, which seemed pretty mild compared to many of the words he could have chosen. I chose something worse.

Paul was now deathly white and had buried his head against Heather. He gabbled a long, never-ending stream of prayer. She wrapped her arms around him and held him tightly, rocking him like a baby.

John reached over for my hand, jaw clenched. His warm, strong grip felt amazing. As though it was protection against anything evil in pursuit of us. Erik sat like stone, tendons in his neck and arms tight as he fought the machine up into the sky. I wanted to bury my face in my freezing fingers, but John's hand felt so good. Would I rather my last memory was of a gorgeous man holding my hand or of the ground racing up to meet me? I kept my eyes open, but as John's gaze flicked sideways my own followed.

A figure with a bushy dark beard burst out from the trees and ran into the open. I saw the spit of shots leaving the barrel of his rifle and flinched as they whistled by somewhere horribly close. They missed the skid this time, and thankfully the cabin, too.

A second or two later another man sprinted from cover, his mouth wide open in a silent scream. Then he leveled his rifle and fired at the first shooter, just as the man dropped onto one knee to steady himself.

In horrible slow motion dark-beard collapsed onto the ground. His much paler friend stopped running, gazed up at us, flung his rifle aside, and raced to the body. Already I could see the blood.

John made some sort of signal to Erik who spun us a hundred and eighty degrees and stopped our climb. We hung there, safe but shocked. "Beefy Haldane," John bellowed.

It was so loud. Everything had happened at such speed we didn't all have our head-sets on. The engine hauling us up into the sky clattered and whined and deafened us. But I'd heard that yell of 'Beefy Haldane' for sure. So did that make the other man Roddy Whitebottom?

I shook Paul's shoulder, trying to get him out of his funk,

knowing his PTSD had taken him over again. Heather shot me a glare and tried to push me away.

"He knows him," I screamed. "I think that's his friend Roddy from Afghanistan."

At that, Paul let go of Heather and stared at me. I laid a hand against his face and made sure he understood me. "Roddy. Your friend Roddy."

He was still white and shaking, his features pinched. I'm sure my freezing hand must have felt more like punishment than comfort.

"Stop it!" Heather demanded, but Erik had sized up the situation and brought us back down again. Beefy Haldane lay dead. Nothing was surer. And the other man was crouched beside him, the picture of contrition.

The Squirrel settled a safe distance from them, but no-one was threatening us now. Beefy had toppled over onto his weapon, and Roddy had thrown his well out of the way.

We scrambled out and trooped across to the sad scene. Paul managed to rally sufficiently to accompany us but was still deathly pale.

"Roddy needs your help and your prayers," I insisted, hauling him along. Heather kept trying to tug him back. What were we even doing outside? This was men's work, Military men's work. A book editor and an actress were surplus to requirements for sure.

"Secure the other weapon," I heard Erik say to John.

Mercifully Ten Ton had high-tailed it right out of the valley to keep his children safe. Just as well.

"Padre," Roddy gasped, recognizing Paul. "He moved. He dropped.... I didn't mean... I only intended to wing him."

He looked so young and so contrite, my heart went out to him. "You saved us all," I insisted. "We saw how it happened."

Roddy bent over double, wrapping his arms around himself as though that could contain the pain and guilt.

"We'd all be dead if you hadn't immobilized him," Erik agreed.

"Killed him," John corrected, inspecting the wound as dispassionately as if it was a melon hit by a spade and not a human head burst apart by a bullet. Cold. The Black Ops thing roared back into my brain and wouldn't be leaving anytime soon. "Nice flying, Jacobsen," he added. "Another few dollars I owe you."

Erik's grimace was nowhere near a smile. He moved beside Heather and slid an arm around her, urging her to turn away from the grisly scene.

Paul laid his hand on Roddy's shoulder. "Shall we pray for his soul?" he suggested, dropping to his knees on the grass beside the shocked and grieving man.

Roddy uncurled, drawing in a huge gulp of air. He touched Beefy's blood-spattered shoulder. "Too much happening all at once for him," he said hoarsely. "After what he went through in Afghan. One chopper arriving here he might have coped with, but when two flew in it was the war all over again." He looked across at Paul. "His father still refused to acknowledge him and then sold the farm, so that was the end of his hopes in that direction."

"No wonder he couldn't kick the drugs," I heard Paul say.

Roddy moved his hand down Beefy's back in a brief caress. "And then he was told his son was killed on the beach. Shot through the heart, execution-style." He turned his gaze up to John. "What did the kid do to deserve that? Steal a bit of pot?"

The rain fell gently over the group of us, diluting the blood from Beefy's hair so it ran down the side of his face. I couldn't look. "We may as well get back into shelter," I suggested.

Erik grunted possible agreement and led Heather away. I watched as he prowled around the helicopter skids and photographed the sites where the bullets had hit. He also, once the rest of us had made our way there, came back and photographed Beefy and the general area.

"I'll stay with him," Roddy said as the rest of us climbed aboard. "Can you...?"

"Doing it now," John said, holding up his phone before scrolling to Bruce Carver.

"I'll stay too," Paul said, pulling himself together with a massive effort. "Won't leave you alone with him." He shivered. His T-shirt was dark where the rain had soaked into the oatmeal-colored cotton.

John reached into a bin and tossed a couple of tightly rolled bundles to them. "Waterproof. We'll get the ladies home next."

Paul and Roddy shook the garments out.

"We'll come back if the cops are going to be a while," he added, returning to his phone call.

Decorating the loquat tree was now the last thing on my mind.

13

CHRISTMAS LUNCH

IT'S a time-honored tradition in Drizzle Bay on the Sunday before Christmas; everyone is welcome at the community lunch provided they bring something to share. It can be as small as a posy of flowers to decorate a table if money is tight... as large as three quarters of a prime Angus cattle beast if that's what the Police find when they search the property of the sister of a man accused of rustling.

After we'd discussed my abduction at the Point, Bruce Carver told me the poor woman was greatly relieved to have her threatening no-good brother in custody and his unsightly big walk-in chiller out of her small back garden.

Butcher Bernie Karaka offered his services to slice the perfectly hung carcass into steaks and roasts for the assorted gas and charcoal barbecues offloaded at the shops by local citizens. He turned the rest into his own special-recipe sausages and patties, which were almost more popular than the steaks.

Lord Jim Drizzle also provided succulent new season's lambs for spit-roasting. Lady Zinnia donated a painting to raffle – and for once I liked it. A dazzling red poinsettia in a pot on a windowsill, with a background that was recognizably Drizzle Farm.

Iona brought an abundance of Christmas cakes and puddings, thanks to Heather's help in her kitchen. Betty McGyver from Horse Heaven rolled up with huge tubs of stewed plums and apricots from her trees. The Mini-mart obliged with commercial-sized containers of ice-cream and gallons of cream and custard.

Wives admired the colorful salads prepared by their neighbors, secure in the knowledge their own creation would be just a little crisper and tastier than any of the others. Husbands brought bottles of home brew to sample and share, and for a couple of hours the liquor licensing laws were relaxed. As indeed were many of the good citizens of Drizzle Bay once the beer started flowing. I've no idea where all the wine came from.

The trestle tables stretched in a double row under the sheltering shop verandas. Christmas carols poured from specially installed speakers, and there was a break for clearing the first course away and setting out the desserts so Paul's special nativity re-enactment could take place.

The Virgin Mary wore less eye make-up than she had during rehearsals. The boy playing Joseph tripped on his long robe and was hauled upright again by a herald angel. The Baby Jesus looked a lot like Barbie swaddled in a shawl, and the ox and ass were wondrous creations decorated by some of the youngest pupils at the local school. One of the dads had cut them out of leftover wallboard. Their hides were an interesting patchwork of old carpet samples. The ass had cat's whiskers. The ox had an udder – which was possibly better than any male alternative a seven-year-old might invent.

Paul was still desperately shaken and distressed, but no-one would have known except Heather and me. The helicopters, the guns, the shots, the blood, and Beefy's death, had all combined to pull his PTSD into horrible sharp focus again. He somehow managed to stay upright and affable, moving quietly among the guests with a greeting and a kind word for everyone. After what he'd recently been through it was a miracle he was still on his feet.

Once the final carols were sung and the clearing up began, we made him sit down with a glass of orange juice and a slice of cake. "You did well, Paul-James,' Heather said, ruffling his hair. No 'product' today, obviously. Her pale fingers moved freely through his dark thatch.

"Sometimes," he said reflectively, "it's good to have some-thing so involving you can't think about other things."

"Just the afternoon family service now," Heather agreed. "And you can glide through that with your eyes closed."

"I'll manage better than gliding," he admonished. "Whole heart or nothing."

"Joking," she murmured as Jim and Zinnia Drizzle stopped by for a word.

"Excellent lunch again this year, Vicar," Jim said. "Wonderful turn-out."

"And the nativity play was charming," Lady Zin added. "I took a few photos. Might manage a painting or two for the school."

"Be sure to get the ox's udder in," I couldn't help suggesting.

She pressed her lips together and her eyes twinkled. "That *was* creative," she agreed.

"Hopefully that's the end of the current round of rustling," Jim said. "The end paddock by the road is a little too accessible. I'll get Denny to sort out some extra security once he's back from Fiji. Maybe cameras like the avocado growers are using now."

"So was it your beef we were eating?" I asked. "Some of us assumed it might be Perce Percy's."

Jim shook his head. "Sadly, it was mine. And it seems Haldane had nothing to do with it, despite my suspicions."

"Still no word about who killed the son?" Zinnia asked. "Horrible the way he was laid out on that tree."

"Still no word," I agreed. "Bruce Carver is convinced it wasn't those rustlers who moved in to the cottage at the Point and bailed up poor Margaret. They swear they found him already dead. Admitted they put him on the tree, though, because they were fed up with him stealing their pot."

"Twisted," Zinnia muttered.

"Or high," I said. "They thought they'd make an example of him in some warped way. The DS said the bullet didn't come from any of their guns."

"But they did steal his motor bike," Paul said. "The Police found it parked beside the chiller in the sister's garden."

Jim nodded. "I saw that in the Coastal Courier."

Little did they know I'd written the article. After seeing so many of the people I edited turning up in print I'd decided to join them. I quite enjoyed keeping my ears flapping and writing up short (unpaid) reports for Bob Burgess the editor. The crafting conference and sale had set me on a whole new path.

The nativity play and the community lunch would probably feature in the first January issue. I'd taken photos in case no-one else had.

The new garbage bins on the beach that Graham's Rotary Club had raised funds for deserved a mention.

Then there was the Burkeville's second helicopter and John's action adventures. Also Lurline Lawrence's story about the incredible trek little Theo the miniature dachshund had made as he tried to return to his owners (on such short legs, too).

Winston Bamber had scored an art-world coup – an upcoming exhibition of works by the talented Rona Costello-Eckhardt – better known as 'Old Rona Jarvis' to Drizzle Bay-ites. In late spring, when Paul and Jasper Hornbeam had helped clear up her overgrown garden and mended her unsafe steps they'd found a treasure trove of 1960s psychedelic and op art stacked in her disused garage. The sale of just a few pieces at Winston's eye-watering prices would assure Rona of full-time care for the rest of her life.

Belinda Buttercup had let slip to me she'd be taking over Drizzle Bay Modes in a couple of months. She planned to demolish part of the wall between the two premises and start a mother-of-the-bride business to complement Brides by Butterfly. Good idea!

Everywhere I looked, and everyone I spoke to, seemed to have a story. Don't ever tell me nothing happens in tiny towns...

Meanwhile we still had our murder mystery. Bruce Carver's fingernails were now so short he had nothing left to chew. There was no murder weapon, no motive, and no apparent suspect as Christmas came and went. Who had killed poor Beefy junior? And why?

———

I BUMPED into Jim Drizzle quite by chance ten days into January as I was heading to the Mini-mart for a few groceries. He was sitting at one of Iona's outdoor tables with a cuppa and a big slice of chocolate cake.

"Uncle Jim!" I exclaimed. "What are you doing eating that when Lady Zinnia cooks so well?"

He looked as guilty as a dog caught stealing sausages off a barbecue, and motioned me to sit. "Zin doesn't put frosting on anything or make puddings these days," he confided. "She's trying to keep our weight down, but I've a bit of a sweet tooth. Be happy to go without a dozen crackers and cottage cheese for just one slice of this occasionally."

"Might need to be *two* dozen crackers and cottage cheese, I said, eyeing the decadent cake. "I won't tell her. In fact it looks so good I'll grab a piece for myself if you're going to be here a few minutes longer." I ducked inside and was soon back again. It was indeed very good cake.

"No more stock stolen?" I asked, licking crumbs out of my lipstick.

"All good so far. I've got Denny coming back from Fiji today so that'll take a load off."

I wiped my fingers on the paper napkin. "The wedding went well, I hope?"

"He phoned to say it had, and to check on things generally. It sounds as though Lorraine is going downhill fast, though. The extra holiday time hasn't helped."

I did some slow, sympathetic nodding. "Maybe it's just as well the daughter hurried the wedding up if his wife's getting worse?"

Jim shook his head. "Or maybe it would have been a lot less stress for her if young Caitlin had left things the way they already were."

I shrugged. "Hard to tell. Difficult either way. Denny was a friend of Graham's. I used to adore him from afar when I was twelve or so. I guess he must have been about eighteen."

Jim gave a comfortable chuckle. "You were a little minx

back then. I remember your dad being worried about what he had to look forward to."

I looked at old Jim with astonishment. "No, surely not! I was quite a good kid. I teamed up with Duncan pretty early on, but it never came to much back then. We went our separate ways for years and then met up again." I screwed up my paper napkin as though I was screwing Duncan Skeene's neck. "More's the pity."

We sat there in the sun, silent for a couple of minutes.

Suddenly Jim took a determined breath and said, "I'm going to get rid of that tree."

"Where David Haldane was laid out?"

He gave a slow nod. He must have known I was behind some of the Courier's stories because he added, "I don't want this getting around until it's done, Merry. *Fait accompli* and so on."

"Okay, but why?"

Jim turned his cup on its saucer, plainly looking for the best explanation. "It's not quite on my land," he admitted after a few seconds. "It's probably not my business to see to it, but I don't like the thought of having it there after what happened. And everyone will have a different theory about what's best to do; cut it up with chainsaws, dig a pit with a dozer and try to bury it..."

"Have to be a huge pit," I interrupted.

His bristly white eyebrows rose. "Or blow it to smithereens with explosive. That's the option I'd favor. We've got some left in the safe out in the barn. From clearing the tree slash June's big storm dumped into the river from the forestry land. Heck of a mess, that was."

"Sounds pretty effective."

"Put a few sticks underneath and up she goes."

"What? You don't have to drill holes first?"

Jim gave a bark of laughter. "Denny's the farm manager. His decision. That's what I pay him for." After a few more seconds he pushed his chair back from the table. "I dropped my Lizzie off with Lisa for a health check earlier. I'll go and collect her now. Nice to see you Merry." He tipped his shapeless old stockman's hat to me and stumped away.

Hmm. Definitely a story for the Courier if I could keep it to myself and maybe get some before and after photos. And during!

I dived into the Mini-mart for the groceries, did a quick trek around the shelves, and then settled at my desk intending to put in some serious work. The current project was a dual-time novel with sixties mini-skirts, go-go boots and flared trousers in places and the Second World War years in others. That era's really trending right now. The heroine – or possibly her mysterious mother – moved back and forth in time, and it was a satisfying puzzle, both to read and to work with.

On such a fantastic day a beach-walk with the spaniels was definitely on, so once I'd had enough of Pearl Harbor, utility clothing, far-off gunfire and missing sweethearts, I decided to complete the beach walk the rustlers had so rudely interrupted. It would be a chance to see how

Margaret was, and to take some sneaky 'before' photos of the huge white washed-up tree. Thoroughly pleased with that plan I made a few dinner preparations, and once the sun was past the hot middle of the afternoon, I locked up the house, whistled the dogs over, and attempted to attach their leads. They know what that means! Unfortunately it makes them so excited that getting the clips anywhere near their collars can be a major job.

"Come here, you silly boy," I crooned to Manny as he lunged at me and then galloped off again. "You're not making things easy," I complained, pursuing him for a few steps and using that as a ruse to grab sideways for Dan's collar instead.

"Good boy, *such* a good dog," I told Dan, as he pranced up on his hind legs, bouncing as though he was on springs. I scratched the top of his head and stroked his ears, leading him over toward the gate once I had his lead clipped on. Was Manny going to be left out? Not if that treatment was on offer! I ignored him until we were right by the gatepost. Graham has screwed a handy big hook onto it so we can secure a lead there while catching the second dog. I hung the lead there and grabbed for Manny. Victory was mine. They never learn.

Off we went in the Focus, all the way down Drizzle Bay Road, around the bend past Drizzle Farm, and to the end where the old cottage is. There was no sign of the Mini, either parked outside or when I sneaked a glance through the garage window. So much for seeing how Margaret was – hale and hearty and out on the road, apparently.

The spaniels enjoyed a sniff around the yard – probably the scents from the big hunting dogs remained, and no doubt Pierre's perfume, too. Seeing no need to go back to the public access track, I shortened my walk by taking Margaret's route through the end of the garden and down the dry sandy slope where the scruffy maritime plants grew in ankle-grabbing abundance.

John might feel confident letting his shepherds run free but I knew from experience the spaniels could depart at speed in totally different directions so the leads stayed on as I walked along the firm sand as briskly as their questing noses allowed me to.

It took about ten minutes to reach the tree lying beached and bleached in the summer sun. I walked more and more slowly the closer I got, feeling silly about that, and knowing quite well David's body had been gone for several weeks now. It was still hard to get that aerial shot out of my memory though. The absolutely distressing way he'd been displayed. The symmetry. The effect of a crucifixion.

The waves crashed and roared, and somewhere high above me at least one skylark trilled and warbled non-stop. How can such a tiny bird manage that much volume? I heard farm machinery, too. It was a really good summer – probably grass being cut for silage, or hay being bailed. Then, right by the fence dividing Drizzle Farm from the beach a huge green John Deere tractor rumbled to a stop. I hadn't seen it until the last moment because of the way the beach sloped up and then the farmland levelled out.

The spaniels decided a good bark at the intruder was called for, and that's probably what drew the attention of the driver as he climbed down from the high cab. It was Denny McKenzie, my old teenage crush, and now with a lot of silver threaded through his bright red hair. He looked shattered.

I raised a hand. "Denny." And then thought to lower my sunglasses so he could see me better. "It's Merry – Graham's sister."

He pushed his own glasses up and squinted against the bright light and the sparkling sea.

The spaniels continued to bark, and then suddenly fell silent as they found something smelly in the sand to investigate.

"Merry," he said, scratching his head. "What brings you right along here?"

I was hardly going to tell him I wanted to sneak some photos of a tree where a dead man had been laid out. "I came to check on Margaret at the cottage along there," I said, waving in the direction of the Point. "And then decided on a walk. Did Jim tell you about the kidnapping?"

"Not yet. Things on my mind. Catching up with the local happenings will follow 'as and when'."

"Fair enough," I said. "He mentioned the wedding went off well." I hesitated, choosing my words with care. "And that it was tiring for Lorraine."

Denny slid his sunglasses on again, maybe to hide his emotions. "Tiring's one way of describing it. She's weak and weary. I think a wedding's challenging under any circumstances, but when the bride insists on switching all the plans at a couple of weeks' notice, and her mother's critically ill, it's... tough."

"Denny, I'm so sorry."

None of his eighteen-year-old glamor remained now. He was a middle-aged man with the worries of the world on his shoulders.

"But Fiji was nice?" I asked.

He ambled toward me and surprised me by putting a hand on a post and vaulting over the farm fence to the beach. Still athletic, obviously.

"Fiji was paradise. Hot, fine, green and beautiful. Everything the travel brochures say. The wedding was out on the sand, all of us barefoot, if you can believe it."

"Would save buying wedding shoes," I suggested with a grin.

He snorted at that. "The wedding shoes were already bought. Oh well, we'll only be doing it once." He took a couple more steps and stopped, scanning slowly from left to right. "What happened to the boy?"

I presumed he meant David Haldane. "No-one... really... knows. He just turned up dead on the tree. So Jim's already asked you to get rid of it?"

Denny nodded, kicking at the sand with a scuffed boot. "I didn't put him on the tree. That's down to someone else."

A prickle of awareness stole down my spine. David hadn't been discovered until Denny and his family had left for Fiji. So...? "How did you even know about him?" I blurted. I looped the spaniels' leads around a fence post so they wouldn't distract me.

He stayed silent for a few seconds. "Silly young fool," he said.

"You knew he'd died? Before you left?"

"Saw it happen." That was said very reluctantly.

So once again it looked as though I'd be phoning DS Bruce Carver. And once again he wouldn't be pleased with me.

"But how?" I asked. "Who did it? While you've been away the Police have been combing the district for information. They've not made much progress at all, as far as I know."

Denny kicked at the sand again. "He came along the beach on a dirt bike," he said, staring into the distance and taking no notice of me. "All the way from Devon Downs, I reckon. Avoiding the roads. Didn't want to be seen."

To my horror Denny took a few more steps, planted his butt on the tree, and sat knees-apart with his hands hanging loosely between them. You could pay me a million dollars and I wouldn't sit there. Euw.

His gaze wandered far away, up into the hills. "The kid had an old .22," he said. "Taking pot-shots at rabbits, I think. Not that he'd find many along here. But the silly young fool was travelling with it loaded, slung over his shoulder on that bike. He pulled up when he saw me. I had the new tractor pretty much where it is now, and he stopped to admire it." Denny looked across at the huge gleaming machine.

I hate to think how much a big beast like that costs, although probably not as much as Erik's new Squirrel.

"So he hopped off and came toward the fence," Denny continued. "Pretending he was the Great White Hunter, aiming the rifle at fence-posts, that tree trunk over there, imaginary rabbits. It never occurred to me either of us was in danger." He took a long, slow breath. "And he tripped on a piece of driftwood. Not looking where he was going of course. Too busy sighting along the barrel."

I saw Denny swallow before he continued.

"When he started to fall, he somehow released the safety and yanked back on the trigger. The shot hit the loader arm and ricocheted straight back at him."

Denny raised a hand, pushed his sunglasses up, and covered his eyes with one hand. Clutched his chest with the other. "Got him right here."

I stood, silent and shocked, remembering the bullets hitting the helicopter skids on the day we filmed the TV commercial. In truth I was going to carry that memory with me forever. At least they'd bounced away harmlessly after the frightening impacts.

"Why didn't you tell anyone?" I whispered.

He shook his head. "Dead instantly. Got himself right in the heart. There was nothing I could do, Merry, except get the heck away and take my family safely to Fiji so we could see Caitlin married while Lorraine was still alive." He uncovered his eyes and looked straight at me before the sunglasses fell down into place again. Weary brown eyes, filled with pain. "I didn't want any hold-ups. We were cutting it horribly fine already but I'd needed to block a piece of the boundary where thieves had got in. Hence I had the big bucket on the tractor so I could pile some rocks up. You can see the nick in the steel where the arm was hit."

"Oh Denny..."

"Yeah – not a good set of circumstances. The boy lying dead. Me being hassled to get to the airport to fly out. Caitlin the bridezilla to beat them all. Lorraine almost dying on her feet and trying to hang on bravely. I couldn't help him, but I could help my family get through the wedding madness so that's what happened."

"You should have told someone."

He grimaced. "I was barely keeping my nose above water. Hanging onto my sanity by a thread. Jim let me know they'd found him when I rang. Found him up here on the tree," he added, patting the smooth wood. "That wasn't where I left him, and there was no way he could have got up by himself, so someone interfered with him. Why didn't *they* let the cops know? I wanted to be back here with my wife safe before I put myself in jeopardy for something that was none of my fault."

"It was Beefy Haldane's son," I said.

His eyebrows rose above his sunnies. "Had about as much sense as his father, then."

I shook my head. "Beefy's dead too. I saw it happen."

This time it was Denny's turn to try and console me. He held out a big hand, and for some reason I took it, and I also took a step or two closer to the awful tree and leaned on it, even without being given the million bucks.

The spaniels started to whine and fuss and I clicked my tongue at them. "I was in a chopper with some other people. Beefy came galloping out of the bush, screaming and shooting. I think he thought he was back in Afghanistan."

"What a mess."

I nodded, and let out a long, slow sigh. "Okay with you if I phone the cops? DS Bruce Carver, who I know a bit? They're going mad trying to work out who shot this boy. All they know so far is that the men who heaved him up onto the tree weren't the ones who killed him. Wrong guns."

"Jim's asked me to get rid of this tree," Denny said, avoiding my question. "That's what I'm doing here. Working out what needs to be done. Not anything else."

I kept hold of Denny's hand as I dug my phone out of my pocket and scrolled for Bruce Carver with my thumb, hoping for once he'd be there.

"Ms Summerfield," he grated. "What a pleasant surprise. What would you like to tell me this time?"

If I could have reached through the phone and slapped his snarky face, I would have. However, it was going to give me almost more pleasure to tell him he could stop looking for the murderer because I knew how David had died. "It would be good if you could come out to Drizzle Farm and talk to Denny McKenzie."

"You're saying Denny McKenzie knows what happened?"

"He's just come back from his daughter's wedding in Fiji

and he'll show you where a bullet hit the big loader arm of his tractor and bounced back and hit David. David effectively shot himself – not that he meant to."

There was total silence from the phone for several seconds.

"I'm right here on the beach with Denny. He's just told me. Would you like me to send you a photo of the impact?" I raised an eyebrow at Denny and squeezed his hand. The poor man was white as a ghost. "Tomorrow, maybe? His wife's extremely unwell."

"Could I speak with him?"

I gave Denny an apologetic glance, held out my phone, let go of his hand, and took the spaniels for a short walk to give him some privacy. The last thing I heard was Denny saying, "Yeah – in the gun-safe at home."

EPILOGUE

"I'LL PICK you up in ten minutes," Paul said. "No point taking two cars."

"Or using twice the petrol," I agreed. "Bye."

Ten minutes. Time to do really good smoky eyes and attempt an elegant up-do with my abundant hair. Heather makes it look so easy – she lifts and twists and then pushes that comb-thing in and it's all tidy and stays that way. I'm more of a messy bun girl, and after a couple of French twist attempts I knew I'd be giving in and making a messy bun again.

The doorbell rang sooner than I expected. I ran a brush through my hair a couple of times and raced to the front door. Already the spaniels had heard the giveaway noise and were barking their displeasure at not having a visitor at the back gate. *Their* gate. Bad luck, I'd give them a good long walk later.

I swung the door open and found Paul. Early. He must have been ready to leave when he rang; there's no way the vicarage is ten minutes away from here. Not even ten minutes on foot.

His smile of greeting was surprisingly shy. "Are you wearing it down?" he asked.

"This?" I asked, grabbing a double handful of hair and flapping it like wings.

He nodded. "It's not windy."

He looked so hopeful I grinned and said, "What *is* it with men and long hair? I was brushing it out for another attempt at making it look like Heather's."

"No..." he said, eyes suddenly darker and more intense. " Leave it like that. And let me brush it."

"What?" The late Sally Summerfield would be rolling her eyes at my rude reaction.

"Let me brush it," he repeated, taking a step inside. In that instant he turned from dependable friend and parish vicar to someone else entirely. The hot man I'd had occasional glimpses of had broken through the careful screen we'd always kept between us.

Or had we? Maybe I'd been sending signals when I hadn't intended to? Perhaps he'd seen the admiring glances I'd given his very good legs that first time I found him painting the railings outside Saint Agatha's? Or he knew I'd enjoyed myself a little too much on the evening we'd gone to the Burkeville to make it look as though he definitely wasn't gay?

He'd been happy enough to hold my hand for the TV filming, and he'd slid his arm around my waist of his own volition and not removed it until we broke apart for lunch. Had Paul been quietly courting me while I hadn't noticed?

Clamping my teeth onto my bottom lip, I turned and walked back toward my bedroom. Paul in my bedroom! But there'd definitely be no hanky-panky today. I'd already waved to Heather who was waiting in the car. She'd expect both of us back straight away.

Silently I handed him my big hairbrush and stood in front of the mirror so I could watch him. In our joint reflection I saw how much taller than me he was. How his bicep swelled below the short sleeve of his navy polo shirt as he lifted the brush and drew it down through my long, thick hair with evident pleasure.

How he closed his eyes for a few seconds and inhaled before he resumed brushing. There was nothing exotic about my fruity shampoo but then I saw him bow his head and bury his nose against the strands for a deeper sniff.

After another half dozen slow, careful strokes he said, "Beautiful hair. First thing I noticed about you." Then he caught my eye in the mirror, laid down the brush with obvious reluctance, and said, "Better go."

I locked up the house in a kind of dream. Paul had done that? And I'd let him?

Beefy Haldane's death and Paul's traumatic reaction to the gunfire were a month in the past. He seemed fine. Business as usual. Or was it his iron will and unflagging self-discipline holding him together? I really couldn't tell.

It was now late January. Pupils were pouring back to school. The Coastal Courier had run the story about the demolition of the huge tree on the beach. They had their own before-and-after photos, but it was my spectacular shots of the actual explosion that had grabbed the most space. Bob Burgess had been hopping mad I was the only one who knew exactly when to turn up for the photo shoot.

"Friends in high places," I'd said, tapping the side of my nose. But it hadn't been Lord Drizzle. It was Denny who'd given me the time and date – maybe as thanks for easing the way with Bruce Carver. Not that I'd done much apart from making the initial phone call and explaining the circumstances and the stress Denny had been under. Was still under. Poor Lorraine was clinging grimly to life.

But today was intended for happier things. We were off to the Burkeville for a repeat of Heather's first brunch there before she headed back to England. Her time in Drizzle Bay had rocketed by.

"Hiya!" she said as Paul opened the car door for me. "Look!" She thrust out an arm in my direction. "That's a genuine suntan. Who'd have thought? Pale old me."

"It's a good summer. Nice for you to get outdoors. We'll miss you."

She didn't reply, and I thought that indicated regret. "How do they feel the TV commercial is working?" I asked to fill the uncomfortable silence.

She shrugged. "We'll get an update in a few minutes. I know they've been busy."

I was sure they had. Now my ears were tuned to even the faintest note of a helicopter and I often wondered, when I heard them in the distance, if Erik was dropping a load of adventurers off with John, or if he was collecting wealthy tourists to show them some of his secret and most spectacular beauty spots.

Paul pulled into the parking lot. We were earlier than most of the crowd, and Erik came out from behind the counter, showing us to the same table we'd had brunch at the first time. "Continuing the tradition," he said when I expressed surprise.

"Good tradition," Heather murmured.

From behind the fence Fire and Ice added their own comments. I heard John's distinctive whistle and they fell silent again.

Brunch was fancier this time. Glasses and a carafe of juice were already arranged in the center of the table. A small jug held some pretty flowers.

Paul and I sat. Erik slid his hand down Heather's arm before pulling out her chair and making it plain the one next to it was his.

"Same as the first time?" he asked.

"You can't have remembered what we all ate," I protested.

He narrowed his eyes. "Try me." And sure enough the same choices were soon set down in front of us.

"Is he doing his party trick?" John asked as he joined us

with the final two plates. "This guy has a memory like nothing you can imagine. Tell him once and it's in his brain forever."

"Yeah, I don't forget anything important." Erik glanced sideways at Heather, his lips quirking. "Haven't forgotten anything about you."

I saw Paul sit up a little straighter. He almost bristled.

"How are the heli-tours going?" I asked, hoping to dispel any tension.

Erik kept his gaze fastened on Heather as he said, "Swell. More successful than we expected this early. Good future ahead."

I thought of Paul watching me in the mirror as he brushed my hair. Had he looked at me that intensely? As though he could ignite me with a glance or a touch?

Heather picked up her fork. Bowed her head. Was she saying grace or was she avoiding Erik's incendiary gaze?

HE REACHED ACROSS and took the fork from her with one hand. Tilted her chin up with the other so she had to look at him.

"Stay," he said. "Change your booking."

Her lips parted and her brow furrowed. "What for?"

There was a moment's absolute silence. I swear the surf stopped roaring and the coffee machine noise died away and there was no more clatter of knives and forks on plates.

He slid his hand in under her jaw so she couldn't look away. His black eyes were more serious than I'd ever seen them. "Me."

THE END

A NOTE FROM KRISTIE

KRISTIEKLEWES.COM

Thank you so much for choosing to read my book! And thank you even more if you write a review.

I want to acknowledge here the encouragement of two of my writer friends, Diana Fraser and Shirley Megget. We've been making each other laugh for a very long time and initially planned to write cozy mysteries as a threesome so we could produce books faster for you.

But life gets in the way sometimes and we each got tied up with other projects. However, Shirley keeps poking plot-lines in my direction and I can't resist taking over and embroidering them. MURDER IN THE AISLE was the first. Then this one – XMAS MARKS THE SPOT. MURDER! THEY MEOWED followed. (There's an excerpt of that just below.) Then we have BODY! THEY BARKED. To see the other Kristie Klewes cozies, go to kristieklewes.com I'd also like to thank my author friend Serenity Woods for reasons too numerous to mention. I'm sure you'd love her Avalon Cafe series.

Big thanks as well to the members of my local chapter of Romance Writers of New Zealand, and The Ngaio Writers Group. It's great to have people to bounce ideas off.

And most of all, I want to thank my husband, Philip. He's so good at putting up with my eccentric queries and late dinners and computer hassles.

———

I began my working life as an advertising copywriter at my local radio station. After saving up enough, I lived in Italy and London. Then I returned to my capital city of Wellington and worked in TV, radio again, several advertising agencies, and spent happy years as a retail ad manager. Totally hooked on fabrics, I followed this by going into business with Philip as a curtain installer, working for some of the city's top designers. Quite a turnaround! It was finally time to write fiction. In twenty years I haven't fallen off my ladder once through drifting into romantic dreams, but I've certainly seen some beautiful homes and met wonderful people, some of whom I may just have stolen glimpses of for the books.

Now read on for a taste of number three!

Thank you,

Kristie.

BOOK 3 – MURDER! THEY MEOWED – JUST A TASTE

THERE'D NEVER BEEN a whisper about Matthew Boatman being a hoarder. Dapper bespectacled Matthew – who always mowed his small front lawn with a push-mower, and was often seen clipping his six privet bushes into perfect globes. Woe betide any rogue shoot trying to spoil their perfection.

It seemed odd, on the day when I was collecting for the Red Cross, that his front door swung open when I knocked and a cat gave a loud and plaintive yowl from somewhere around head height.

"Matthew," I called, pushing the door further open after no-one had appeared after thirty seconds or so. Maybe he was in the bathroom? Perhaps he'd just popped inside from a snipping expedition to make a cup of tea?

The cat yowled again. Then there was a blur and a loud thump, followed by the rapid tattoo of furry feet on bare floor-boards. The cat had gone. But where had it been? I took a step forward, waiting for my eyes to adjust to the dimness.

It was very dark inside after the bright sunny day. Drizzle Bay in springtime can be dazzling. Blue skies, hard, low sun. I took another step. Something crunched under my foot.

I bent down to see what I'd damaged, and the light from the doorway behind me revealed the head of a small bird. Euw! The body had been eaten, and a swirl of grey-brown feathers drifted along the narrow hallway. Narrow, I realised an instant later because the walls on either side were stacked solid with old newspapers and magazines. The head-high barricade ran past closed doors and blocked access to those rooms. The cat must have been perched on top. No wonder it had made a thump as it jumped down.

There were no other sources of light. No doors open, so no windows illuminating anything from the outside. No lamps on. Just a faint glow from the far end of the right angled paper-stacked space.

"Matthew!" I really bellowed that time. This was weird and spooky. I didn't like it at all. My hair was up in a pony-tail and the back of my neck was chilled and prickling as the little hairs there rose up.

My voice brought no human reply, but another cat howled. I'm sure it was a different animal because its voice was low and raspy, unlike the high panicked tone of the first one.

This was fairly nasty. Should I call the Police? I stood there dithering for a few moments, then pulled out my phone, turned its torch on, and took three or four resolute steps forward. There was an open door behind me only a few yards away, so whatever I found around the bend I could easily escape.

Even so, the heels of my ankle-boots sounded loud on the bare timber floor. Matthew had no carpet, no rugs, nothing to soften the noise of my slow steps.

I peeked around the corner just as at least three cats made a dash for freedom. My torch made their shadows look enormous and distorted against the stacked-paper walls. A tail brushed past my leg, paws raced over my feet and off down the hallway. I'm ashamed to admit I screamed. Only a short, surprised squawk, but still...

Matthew Boatman sat at the cluttered kitchen table, leaning at ease in his chair, a half-opened can of cat-food in front of him. A can opener drooped from the rim.

A long gleaming arrow was neatly imbedded in his back, right between the slats of the chair, but I didn't see that to start with. In fact I was fully into the kitchen, asking him if he was okay, before I noticed it. He definitely had a strange expression on his face.

I imagine I did too, as I bolted for freedom every bit as fast as the cats had, dropping my Red Cross collection bag as I ran. The coins inside made a loud clunk on the floorboards and some of them escaped and rolled away into the darkness.

I sagged against the front gate for a bit of support, switched off my torch, and scrolled for DS Bruce Carver's number. The cheerful yellow jacket I'd put on to match the tubs of daffodils in the main street of the village suddenly seemed a very untasteful choice.

"Ms Summerfield," the DS said, sounding surprised to hear from me. Well, it had been ages since I'd had to tell him he should go to Drizzle Farm and have a word with Denny McKenzie about the body on the tree. Maybe he hadn't expected to hear from me again? For sure I hadn't imagined I'd ever find a third body in our sleepy village.

Made in United States
North Haven, CT
01 September 2024

56816692R10150